STRIKEFORCE AGENT
VALERIE INGLEWOOD

BAD MOON RISING

T.K. WILDE

Dreamstone Publishing © 2016

www.dreamstonepublishing.com

ISBN: 1925499235

ISBN-13: 978-1-925499-23-0

Disclaimer

This is a work of fiction. Any resemblance to persons living or deceased is purely coincidental, and is not intended.

Dedication

To my readers – without you, there would be no stories.

To all of my family and friends, who support me when I am writing, and make it possible for books to get finished – thank you!

Table of Contents

Chapter 1 1

Chapter 2 11

Chapter 3 23

Chapter 4 33

Chapter 5 43

Chapter 6 53

Chapter 7 63

Chapter 8 73

Chapter 9 83

Chapter 10 95

Chapter 11 107

Chapter 12 117

About the Author... 125

Other Books in the Valerie Inglewood Series .... **Error! Bookmark not defined.**

Here is your preview of Book 2 in the series 127

Chapter 1 129

Other books from Dreamstone Publishing 138

Chapter 1

Valerie Inglewood held her rifle out of the dirt and crawled behind the bunker. She wedged the rifle into her shoulder and took careful aim at the man hiding behind the bush. The crackle of gunfire echoed from the other side of the woods and set her nerves on edge. Were her comrades alive over there? She couldn't think about them right now. She steadied her breathing and inched her finger closer to the trigger.

The man jumped three feet into the air when she pulled the trigger. Her rifle jammed against her shoulder, but she ignored the pain and steadied her weapon. The man whirled around, but before he could get his own weapon into position, Valerie fired again. The shot hit in square in the chest, and he toppled backward into the dirt.

Valerie choked on the dust when she slithered forward and crouched over his prostrate form. Yes, he was well and truly dead. She caught sight of a string of camouflaged shapes slipping through the trees. Were they her friends, or were they enemies?

All at once, an air horn sounded behind her. She sat back on her heels and poked the man on the ground in the ribs.

"That's the bell. You can get up now."

He sat up and spat dust out of his mouth. Then he pushed his goggles back on his head. "That was some fine shooting, Val. I didn't even see you there."

"Of course you didn't see me, Rex," Valerie teased. "You were too busy scratching your backside."

He laughed. Giant orange spatters dotted his chest and back. "You always were a crack stalker."

They stood up together and slapped each other on the back. Then they strolled back across the course to the locker room. Valerie hung up her fatigues and helmet and set her rifle in the locker.

"Do you have any plans for dinner tonight?"

"None that I know of," Valerie replied.

Rex started to say something else when a tall woman with flaming red hair hanging down her back stepped into the locker room. Snake skin cowboy boots showed under the hems of her tight blue jeans.

"Charlene Brockworth!" Rex obviously knew her....

Charlene shook Valerie's hand. "In the flesh. Sorry to interrupt your session, but you're coming with me. We have a case to investigate."

Valerie glanced around the locker room. "Right now? I've got a debrief with my team. I can't miss that."

"No time like the present." Charlene waved her hand toward the door. "We've got a suspicious electrocution at the Mackenzie Hunting Lodge."

"But that's all the way up near the Wyoming state line," Valerie replied. "

"That's right." Charlene held the door open. "So we better get going. We've got a long drive ahead of us."

Valerie exchanged glances with Rex, but Charlene was already out the door and around the corner out of sight. Valerie grabbed her duffel bag and hurried after her. Charlene led the way to the parking lot.

Before Valerie could say anything, she found herself buckled into the passenger seat of a trim sedan, hurtling down the highway heading north, out of Denver. Charlene gripped the steering wheel in a choke hold. She shot Valerie a wry grin. "Welcome to Strikeforce."

Valerie hooted. "That's some welcome. I never even knew I was selected to the team, and now I'm on my way north to solve my first case with Charlene Brockworth."

"Is that so bad?" Charlene asked.

"Are you kidding?" Valerie asked. "I dreamed of this job all the way through the Academy. I worked my tail off to earn the top spot in my class so I'd have a chance to try out for this position. The Strikeforce Investigation Team is the most elite law enforcement unit in the western United States. I heard three hundred people applied for this job."

"That's true," Charlene replied. "And I interviewed every single one of them."

Valerie's head whipped around. "You interviewed them? You didn't interview me."

"I didn't have to interview you," Charlene replied. "I could tell from your application form that you would get the job. I let Harvey Wilkins interview you instead so I could watch your try-out."

Valerie shook her head. "I would have given everything I had if I'd known you were watching me."

Charlene laughed. "That's exactly why I didn't want you to know I was watching. My reputation precedes me, and I didn't want to muddy the process by showing my hand. No one knew this position was for my partner"

"I wish I had known," Valerie murmured.

"What would you have done differently?" Charlene asked. "You beat fifty of the best applicants in the hundred-meter sprint, and you out-shot them all on the rifle range. You trampled them all in your written essay, and you tested higher than all of them on your investigation assay. You're only the second woman selected to the team, after me. How could you have improved on that if you'd known you were going to be my partner?"

"I don't know," Valerie replied, "but I would have done it. I would have fallen over myself to impress you."

Charlene grinned. "You already impressed me, so you can stop trying now. You got the job, and now you're my partner. We're on our first case together, so now you can impress me with your field skills."

"What do you know about the case?" Valerie asked.

Charlene shrugged. "Not a lot. You know how these luxury resorts are. They won't tell you anything about their guests, so we'll have to find everything out for ourselves. All we know is one of their rich guests fell into an electrical panel and fried."

"That doesn't sound suspicious," Valerie remarked.

"It wouldn't be," Charlene replied, "except that the power station room is strictly off limits to guests, and only one man has the key." Charlene handed her laptop to Valerie. "Take a look."

Valerie opened the laptop, and found a folder open, with all the information related to the case. The file had an FBI file heading.

"FBI?"

Charlene laughed. "Some things are even out of their league."

"What's out of their league about it?" Valerie asked. "It looks pretty straightforward to me. The maintenance man had the key. Let's see....one Jeff Everson. He must have let the victim into the power station."

"Not so fast," Charlene interrupted. "You're forgetting one thing."

"What's that?" Valerie asked.

"The identity of the victim," Charlene replied.

Valerie flipped through the documents in the file. "Porteus Patterson? Not the import magnate from Seattle?"

Charlene nodded.

"And not just from Seattle. He's originally from Saskatchewan. He holds dual Canadian/American citizenship, so his death could blow up into a major incident across the border. That's where we come in."

"Now I understand what you mean by being out of the FBI's league." Valerie frowned. "Where's the Coroner's Report? That should be at the top of the file list, but I don't see it anywhere."

"That's because it's not there," Charlene replied. "The Coroner's Office hasn't sent it through yet."

"That's a little odd," Valerie remarked. "We should have had it before we left Denver. How are we supposed to conduct a murder investigation without it?"

Charlene shrugged. "Maybe the Coroner's Office got inundated with bodies and it's just taking them longer to process each case."

"Or maybe," Valerie countered, "someone wants to cover up the details of Porteus's death. If his death was related to his business dealings, people in high places could use their influence to tie up the wheels of justice for...... well, forever."

Charlene peered into her rearview mirror. "I won't argue with that."

"So what do you think about the mode of death?" Valerie asked. "Do you think the maintenance man brought him down to the power station to talk to him and he accidentally stumbled into the electrical panel, or did this Everson character push him into the panel in a fit of rage?"

Charlene burst out laughing.

"Listen to you. You're worse than me. I don't know what to think about the mode of death, but I don't imagine they would call us in if there wasn't something deeper going on. Why would a mere maintenance man kill Porteus Patterson? Look at his employment record. He's been working at the Lodge for five years, and the Lodge is a hundred miles from anywhere he could get to on his day off. He's been stuck in the Rockies all that time with nothing to do but hunt and fish and relax in the woods. He wasn't planted there to kill Patterson."

"It could have been an accident," Valerie suggested. "He could have some reasonable explanation for why Patterson was in the power station room, and Patterson could have bumped into the panel."

Charlene shook her head. "That doesn't explain calling in the Strikeforce Team. This thing goes way deeper than that."

"So what's your theory?" Valerie asked. "Why do you think they called us in?"

"Take a look at this." Charlene took her hand off the wheel and gave the laptop an expert swipe. "It's the guest list."

"But it's all blacked out," Valerie pointed out. "What's that supposed to tell us?"

"Now do you see why they called us in?" Charlene asked.

Valerie stared at the screen. "No."

"It wasn't just Porteus Patterson at that Lodge," Charlene explained. "They couldn't exactly black out the victim's name, could they? But there are other people at that Lodge with big time connections, and they don't want anyone to find out they might be suspected of murder."

"Who said anything about murder?" Valerie asked. "You said it was suspicious. That's all."

"Exactly," Charlene replied. "They would rather pin a murder on a hapless maintenance man than to have word get out that anyone suspected them."

Valerie closed the laptop. "I'm not in Kansas anymore."

"Is that where you're from? Kansas?" Charlene asked.

"I wish I was," Valerie muttered. "I'm from California."

Charlene's head whipped around. "What's wrong with that? I love California."

Valerie rolled her eyes. "You could be the only person in law enforcement who does. Most people get a glazed look in their eyes when I tell them where I'm from. They instantly start telling blonde jokes and asking how I'm going to handle the snow when winter comes."

Charlene glanced over at her. "Which part of California are you from?"

"I'm from Bishop," Valerie replied. "Do you know where that is?"

Charlene nodded. "I sure do, and that explains why you don't have any problem with cold winters. That's a rugged part of the world."

"Thank goodness someone knows it," Valerie replied. "Most people think I'm from Santa Monica or San Diego."

"Beachville," Charlene exclaimed. "So how did you wind up in law enforcement?"

"I always wanted to be a detective," Valerie replied. "When I was a little girl, I wanted to be Encyclopedia Brown. I went to the Police Academy after high school, but then I found out about Strikeforce. I knew I had to get on the team if it was the last thing I ever did."

"Your application said you did mountain rescue, even when you were still in high school," Charlene remarked. "You got three citations for bravery, even when you didn't complete the rescue operations. That means a lot in a place like Bishop."

Valerie's jaw dropped. "You remember that from my application?"

"It was so unusual I had to look it up," Charlene replied. "You risked your life on three separate occasions to rescue people caught in the mountains. You didn't succeed, but you went farther above and beyond the call of duty than anyone else on your team. Your team captain recommended you for honors."

Valerie turned away. The countryside rolled away past her window. "I'm sure some of the other applicants had similar credentials."

"Some of them did," Charlene replied. "But not a lot. Not many people on the mountain rescue team would do what you did."

"I don't know why not," Valerie told her. "I don't know why people join the mountain rescue team if they aren't going to do everything humanly possible to rescue people who need rescuing."

Charlene patted Valerie's knee.

"That's exactly why I chose you to be my partner."

Chapter 2

The car rolled up the long gravel driveway and stopped in front of what looked like an enormous log cabin. Towering pine trees obscured its pitched roof. The instant Valerie and Charlene stepped out of the car, a thin man with a thin mustache ran out and pretty much yanked Valerie's hand off her arm. "Oh, thank God you're here! I've been worried sick ever since.... ever since *it* happened. Thank God you're here at last!"

Valerie extricated her hand from his grip and rubbed the pain out of her fingers. "It's a pleasure to meet you, Mister....."

"Anglesea," he replied. "Allen Anglesea. I'm the owner of the Mackenzie Lodge, and I've been out of my mind ever since.... ever since.... you know."

"It's a pleasure to meet you, Mr. Anglesea," Valerie replied. "I'm Valerie Inglewood, and this is Charlene Brockworth. She's the lead investigator on this case."

Charlene held up both hands. "Not at all. By all means, Valerie, take the lead."

"No way!" Valerie shot back. "Don't you even think of throwing me in the deep end on my very first case"

Charlene laughed. "All right. If you insist. Just let me know if you want to take over."

Valerie snorted. "Not likely with you around."

Allen Anglesea led them into the lodge. Log beams held up the vaulted ceiling, and a solid log formed the bannister of the staircase rising from the main floor. Patterned rugs and leather couches populated the front lobby.

Allen took two keys from behind the reception desk and handed them to Valerie and Charlene. "You two make yourselves at home. You have free access to all the facilities, and a full charge account is open in the dining room for your enjoyment. If there is anything you need, don't hesitate to let me know."

He vanished into the woodwork. Valerie dropped her voice to a whisper. "Are we staying here?"

"Of course," Charlene replied. "This case will take days or maybe weeks to solve. We couldn't exactly commute back and forth to Denver every day."

"But I don't have anything," Valerie pointed out. "I don't even have a clean pair of underwear."

Charlene smiled. "The team will send your things up later today."

"The.... team?" Valerie stammered.

Charlene laid her hand on Valerie's arm. "You're not in Kansas anymore, Dorothy. You won't be living at the Alleycat Boarding House when you get back to Denver. Our team has special quarters in the upper floors of our building downtown. You'll be living there from now on."

"But my things...." Valerie protested.

"The team will move you into the building while you're here," Charlene explained. "You have nothing to worry about. In the meantime, they'll send you a suitcase full of clothes and personal items to use while you're here. Whatever they don't send, the Lodge will provide."

Valerie frowned. "I didn't know it was going to be like this. I like to do things for myself."

Charlene turned away. "You'll get used to it. Our team takes care of its own. Once you get selected to this team, you don't have anything else to worry about for the rest of your career."

"It sounds like a cult," Valerie muttered.

Charlene laughed out loud. "Try it for a little while. If you don't like it and you want to go back to scrubbing toilets at the Alleycat for your living, no one will stop you. But after you've lived in a penthouse and worked on the most interesting cases in the country, you won't want to give it up."

Allen came back. "Can I show you to your rooms?"

"Before you do that," Charlene replied, "we'd like to ask you some questions about the.... the accident. As soon as we get that out of the way, we'll go take a look at the crime scene."

The color drained out of his face. "So soon? Don't you want to settle in first?"

"We like to follow a trail while it's still fresh," Charlene explained.

Allen wrung his hands and moaned.

"Do you really have to question me? I don't know anything. I was standing right here, minding my own business, when that oily man came in and told me Mr. Patterson was dead in the power station room. You could have knocked me over with a feather."

Charlene smiled. "By oily man, I assume you're referring to Jeff Everson, the maintenance man who had the key to the power station."

"Who else could I mean?" Allen shot back. "I don't know why I hired him."

"According to his employment record," Charlene pointed out, "he's been working here for five years. You must have been happy with him up until now."

"Of course I was happy with him," Allen replied. "He did a good job and never caused any problems. But I didn't know he was going to kill somebody - and not just anybody, but Mr. Patterson himself. I could go out of business over this, you know."

Valerie couldn't stop herself from chiming in. "What makes you think he killed Patterson? What motive could he possibly have?"

"How should I know?" Allen exclaimed. "Maybe he liked Mr. Patterson's girlfriend and killed him to get hold of her. Maybe he stole money from Mr. Patterson's room and Mr. Patterson found out about it. Maybe he's been waiting five years to get the signal from his controller to get rid of Mr. Patterson."

"If you really thought any of those reasons was a serious possibility," Charlene interrupted, "you would have called the local police and not us. If there was any chance any of that could be true, Jeff Everson would be in jail right now, not running around your lodge. I don't think he killed Patterson at all."

"But if he didn't do it," Allen wailed, "who did? He's the only one with a key to the power station. He must have done it."

"What about you?" Valerie asked. "He's the maintenance man. He's your employee. You wouldn't give him the only key without keeping a master key for yourself."

Allen's eyes darted back and forth between Valerie and Charlene. "Yeah, but I would never have killed Mr. Patterson. This murder will ruin me."

"No one said anything about murder," Valerie pointed out. "We don't know how Mr. Patterson died."

Allen opened his mouth and closed it again. A film of moisture covered his eyes.

"According to our report," Charlene went on, "Jeff claims he found the body in the power station room. He claims the door was locked from the outside with the body inside. Is that true?"

Allen flapped both his hands from the wrist. "How should I know?"

"Didn't you look?" Charlene asked. "Didn't you go see for yourself?"

"Heavens, no!" Allen gasped. "I don't want to have anything to do with any dead body."

"This is your property," Valerie pointed out. "Didn't you even check to see if his story was true?"

Allen shuddered. "God, no!" Valerie and Charlene exchanged a smile.

"You have a key, just like Jeff," Charlene told him. "We can't accuse him just on the basis of having a key. If we did, we would have to accuse you, too."

"But I keep my key in my office," Allen replied. "No one has access to it but me."

"That makes you a suspect," Charlene pointed out.

"Do you keep your office locked all the time?" Valerie asked.

Allen shifted from one foot to the other. "Not all the time, but...."

"Then anybody could have gone in there," Charlene added. "One of the guests could have gotten the key, taken Mr. Patterson to the power station and killed him, and then locked the door and put the key back."

"None of the guests would have done that," Allen exclaimed.

"Then our only other suspect is you," Charlene concluded.

Allen stared at her. Then his lips began to quiver, but before he could break down completely, a tumult drew their attention to the other side of the room.

The French doors leading onto the patio burst open and a blue-haired matron with a dozen rings on every finger and an astonishing collection of gold chains around her neck swept into the room.

"Anton!" she quavered. "Anton, where are you? I simply must change rooms at once. I can't stand another minute of this. Change my room or cancel my stay!"

Allen bowed to her with a beatific smile on his face, all trepidation gone. "My dear lady, I live to serve you." He stepped behind the reception desk.

The woman stopped in front of the desk, and a gargantuan man with a heavy brow occluding his eyes lurched into the room behind her. A crooked smile spread over his face when he spied the two investigators.

A chill ran up Valerie's spine at the sight of him, but Charlene showed no sign of discomfort.

The woman scanned the two investigators up and down. She took in Charlene's snake skin boots, jeans, and long red hair. She took in Valerie's jacket and slacks and plain brown hair cut in layers around her face.

Did she notice the characteristic bulge in the back of each woman's waist where she wore her service pistol? The woman gave a disgusted sneer and turned back to Allen.

"Now, my dear," he said, "would you like the Penthouse Suite by the pool, or would you like the Presidential Suite adjacent to the spa?"

The woman waved her bejeweled hand.

"Neither of those will do, Anton. You know that. I don't want to be anywhere near that horrid power station. It gives me nightmares. Both those rooms are too near the site of the unfortunate event we discussed yesterday."

Allen nodded. Only the faintest trace of a crack appeared in his impenetrable composure.

"Certainly, my dear. I could give you the Equestrian Room on the west side, overlooking the dressage ring. I'm afraid those are the only rooms I have available at the present. The only other option is to wait until Tuesday when Franklin Rastlin leaves for Provence. Then you could take his suite in the east wing."

The woman gasped. "Tuesday! I can't wait until Tuesday."

Charlene took a step forward. "What about our rooms? You could have one of our rooms, and we could move. Are we near the power station?"

Allen pursed his lips. *"Your* room would never do. Mrs. Cooney requires a much higher standard of accommodation than *you.*" He bit off the last word with a sour twist of his mouth.

The woman scanned Charlene up and down one more time. "Never mind. I suppose I have no choice but to take the Equestrian room."

Charlene took another step toward the desk and put out her hand. "Excuse me. I don't think I've had the pleasure of being introduced. I'm Charlene Brockworth, and this is young lady is Valerie Inglewood. We'll be staying here for a while, and we...."

The woman shot Valerie a withering look. "I hope you two aren't.... you know.... together."

Charlene's eyes flew open. She glanced at Valerie, and then she burst out laughing. "No, no. We're federal investigators. We're here to investigate Porteus Patterson's death."

A light came on in the woman's face. She didn't exactly smile, but at least her face softened. "Oh, I see."

Charlene cocked her head to one side. "I still didn't catch your name."

The woman drew herself up stiff and straight. "I'm Babette Cooney."

Valerie gasped. "You're not related to Bill Cooney, the famous movie star, are you? You're not his wife, are you?"

Babette looked down her long nose at Valerie. "I'm not his wife. I'm his mother."

Valerie's hand flew to her heart. "Oh, I'm so sorry. Please forgive me."

Babette humphed, and her whole neck quivered from the concussion. She waved an imperious hand at Allen, who bowed again, and she swept out of the lobby in a gust of icy wind. Her burly escort trundled after her with the same creepy smile on his face.

Allen scurried after Babette with a key in his hand. He didn't say another word to Charlene and Valerie, and he didn't come back. Charlene sighed. "Well, I guess we better get settled in. We'll just check where our rooms are, and then we'll go inspect the crime scene."

Valerie looked around. "How long are we supposed to stay here?"

"Until we solve the case," Charlene replied. "I hope it doesn't take too long. I can't stand places like this."

Valerie glanced down the hall where Babette disappeared. "She's going to be a son of a gun to interview."

Charlene turned away. "Tell me about it."

Valerie fell into step behind her new partner, and they made their way down the corridor to their rooms. They found two identical rooms right next to each other, both with spa tubs and floor to ceiling windows looking out to the mountains. After they looked at their rooms, they met again in the foyer at the end of the hall. "Now to the crime scene."

Charlene headed down the hall toward the exit, but on the way, she passed a picture window overlooking the pool. A group of guests lounged on the deck. "Let's go question them."

"Don't you want to see the crime scene?" Valerie asked. "What happened to following the trail while it's still fresh?"

"All the suspects are sitting together," Charlene pointed out. "We can question them all at the same time."

"I hope they're not all like Babette Cooney," Valerie murmured.

Charlene faced her. "You did really well out there in the lobby just now. I was impressed."

Valerie blushed. "You have to stop being impressed with me. You'll give me a complex."

Charlene grinned. "I mean it. You're a good investigator. I'm glad to have you along."

Valerie didn't answer. She stared into space somewhere beyond Charlene's shoulder. Charlene frowned. "Valerie?"

Valerie didn't move. Her eyes remained fixed on one spot, and she didn't hear a word Charlene said. Charlene turned around and followed her gaze. On the other side of the foyer, a man stood rooted to the flagstone floor. He stared at Valerie as intently as she stared at him. He wore plain brown canvas work pants and steel-toed boots. He wore his brown hair cropped close to his head, and a five-o'clock shadow darkened the bottom half of his face. His dark brown eyes sparkled out of his face.

Charlene read his appearance in one glance. She rounded on Valerie, and this time, her voice alone snapped Valerie out of her trance. "Valerie, look at me."

Valerie raised her eyes to Charlene's face. "Hmm?"

"Pay attention," Charlene told her, "because I'm only going to say this once."

Valerie gulped. "I'm listening."

"This is your first case with the Strikeforce Team," Charlene told her. "Don't forget you're still on trial here."

"I know that," Valerie replied.

"Then you also know he's under suspicion for murder," Charlene shot back. "Don't go losing your head over some man. You don't know anything about him except that he's the one person who had reasonable access to the victim before he was killed."

"We don't know for certain that Porteus Patterson was killed," Valerie pointed out.

Charlene smacked her lips. "You better pull your head out of the clouds and quick. You're here to investigate a death, not fall over yourself making eyes at the prime suspect."

Valerie pulled her shoulders back. "I wasn't doing that, Charlene."

Charlene whirled away. "I'm finished here."

Valerie hurried after her, but she couldn't take her eyes off the man on the other side of the foyer. She only lost sight of him when Charlene pushed open the swinging doors and went out onto the deck to meet the other guests.

Chapter 3

"I'm Charlene Brockworth, and this is Valerie Inglewood. We're here to investigate Porteus Patterson's death." Valerie listened with only half an ear to Charlene's opening pitch.

Despite her claims of innocence, Valerie couldn't shake the guilt of lying. Charlene was right. She couldn't get that man out of her head. His presence sent a wave of hot lava burning through her being. He could only be Jeff Everson, the maintenance man. No paying guest would dress like that in a place like the Mackenzie Lodge.

What was she doing, staring at him like that? She had to suspect him of murdering Patterson, even though they hadn't yet found evidence of foul play. It was standard investigative procedure. She couldn't clear him until she knew for certain he was innocent of any wrong-doing.

And yet his eyes still burned into her soul, even after he no longer stood in front of her. She recognized something in his intent stare. She hadn't seen that burning expression in any man other than certain Navy SEALS and highly ranked federal marshals. Men with that blazing intent didn't even belong on the Strikeforce Team. They migrated to the highest circles of law enforcement nobility.

What was a man like that doing here, fixing faucets and clearing drains? What was a man like that doing in the back woods of Colorado, reading books and whittling wood on his off days? He'd been here five years, and in that time, he'd proved himself a model employee. Allen had never complained about him once.

How could Valerie ask Charlene about him without incurring another reprimand? If she brought him up, Charlene would accuse her of mooning over him. But all Valerie's preconceptions about the man who'd found Patterson dead evaporated out of her mind. He wasn't the slack-jawed flunky she'd thought he'd be. She could almost believe he was planted here specifically to kill Patterson for some higher strategy.

But he couldn't be involved in anything like that. One look into his eyes convinced Valerie that he never operated from anything but the purest motives. He was a Boy Scout. She stopped short of calling him a cop, since she didn't know for certain if he was one. But he carried the same code of honor as any cop, federal or otherwise. He wasn't a gun for hire. He was a guardian angel. She was never more convinced of anything in her life. She would bet everything she had, even her new job on the Strikeforce Team, on it.

Charlene turned around. "Valerie?"

Valerie blinked. "Hmm?"

Charlene frowned. "Have you heard a word we've said?"

Valerie blushed. "Sorry. I was thinking about the case."

Charlene pursed her lips.

"Are you sure you were thinking about the case and not something else?"

Valerie shook the cobwebs out of her head. "I'm sure. I was definitely thinking about the case."

Charlene waved her hand. "Well, while you were thinking about the case, I've just met three of our fellow guests here. This is Heinrich Wiesenthal, from Germany."

A tall blonde man stood up from the glass picnic table and shook Valerie's hand. "So nice to meet you."

"And this is Dempsey Doolittle." A fat old roaster with a bright red nose tried to rise to shake hands with Valerie, but his enormous thighs got stuck under the table. He wound up lifting the whole table off the ground and then crashing down into his chair with the table on top of him.

"Dempsey, please!" Heinrich exclaimed. "You're an elephant."

Dempsey sat down again. "I'm sorry."

Valerie bent over him. "It's a pleasure to meet you."

"And this is Andrea Bottomly Swain," Charlene concluded. "She's the heiress to the Swain chicken tenders fortune."

Andrea didn't get up. She didn't put out her hand. She didn't move from her chair. She didn't even smile. Only her eyes sunken in their black pits shifted up to Valerie's face and then moved away. Valerie didn't dare hold out her hand to Andrea, either.

"Let's start with you, Mr. Doolittle," Charlene went on. "Can you tell us what brings you to the Mackenzie Lodge."

"Do we have to start with me?" Mr. Doolittle whined. "Why can't you start with one of these others."

"We can start with anybody," Charlene replied. "But we have to start with somebody. I'm sure Andrea and Heinrich don't want me to start with them, either."

"I don't mind." Heinrich spoke in a thick German accent, but he gave both Charlene and Valerie such a pleasant smile Valerie couldn't help but smile back. "You can start with me."

Charlene faced him. "Okay, great. What brings you to the Mackenzie Lodge?"

"I'm staying here while I attend a conference in Denver," he replied.

Charlene cocked her head to one side. "But Denver's a four-hour drive away. You couldn't drive all the way there and all the way back every day."

"I only went twice," Heinrich explained, "once on Friday and once on Monday, and I did indeed drive there in the morning and back in the evening both days. But the conference is over now. I won't make that drive again until I drive to the airport to go home."

"And where is home?" Charlene asked.

"Montreal," Heinrich replied.

Charlene's head shot up. "How long have you been living there?"

"Twenty-five years," he replied.

"What was the conference about?" Charlene asked.

"It was a conference of the Veterinarian's Professional Society," Heinrich replied. "I'm the Member at Large."

"Member at Large?" Charlene asked. "What does that mean?"

Heinrich shrugged. "I'm sure I don't know. All it means to me is that I have to show up to the conferences, but I don't have to come every day."

"So you're a veterinarian," Charlene continued.

"I never was one," he corrected her. "I'm an economist."

Charlene and Valerie exchanged glances. "Then how could you be Member at Large for the Veterinarian's Professional Society?"

"They elected me one," he replied. "That's all."

Charlene's eyes widened. "Okay. Well, moving on to Patterson's death. Where were you when you found out about it?"

"I was in the dining room, eating my lunch," he replied. "Allen came in flapping his hands and moaning in despair. He told us Patterson was dead, and the maintenance man must have killed him."

"Did anyone suggest calling the local police?" Charlene asked.

Heinrich glanced at Andrea. "No one would suggest that. We come up to this lodge to get away from all that."

Charlene frowned. "Away from law enforcement?"

"Away from the sordid world of laws and social conformity and all that," Heinrich explained. "This is our haven from the nasty underside of life."

Charlene stiffened. "You call law enforcement, laws and social conformity the nasty underside of life? That's a heck of a way to look at it."

Heinrich shrugged again and looked the other way.

Charlene took a deep breath. "Did you know Patterson very well?"

"Who among us didn't know Porteus Patterson?" Heinrich asked. "He was the most knowable man in the world."

"I didn't know him," Charlene replied. "I didn't know anything about him other than that he made a million in the shipping business."

"He was so much more than that," Heinrich told her. "He was the most powerful man in the Western world. He wielded more power than the President of the United States."

"Then how come I never heard of him?" Charlene asked.

Heinrich didn't say anything to that. Charlene turned to Dempsey Doolittle. "All right, Mr. Doolittle. You've had your reprieve. Now it's your turn. What brings you to the Mackenzie Lodge?"

Dempsey puffed out his enormous chest. "I'm hunting. Isn't that what most people come up here to do?"

"Tell us about your typical day hunting," Charlene told him. "I guess you go out in an SUV to find the...."

"SUV?" Dempsey snorted. "I don't go out in any SUV."

"How do you go out?" Charlene asked. "Do you go by helicopter?"

"I go on horseback," Dempsey replied. "It's the only way to hunt. Everything else is for wannabes."

Charlene's mouth fell open. "You.... go on horseback?"

"Of course I do," he replied. "I've always hunted on horseback."

Charlene scanned him up and down. "Aren't you a little......?"

"A little what?" Dempsey asked.

"I don't know," Charlene stammered. "Aren't you a little out of shape for horseback riding?"

Dempsey patted his bulging stomach. "I'm not as spry as I used to be, but I can still sit a horse as well as ever."

Heinrich turned to him. "I haven't seen the horse alive who could carry a sausage like you."

Valerie couldn't stop herself from choking back laughter. Even Charlene had to bite her lip to stop herself from falling apart. Andrea indulged in a hint of a smile, but she turned away just as fast.

Dempsey frowned and faced Charlene. "You asked what I'm doing here, and I told you."

"Okay. You're hunting," Charlene went on. "How often have you gone hunting since you've been here?"

"I've been every day," Dempsey told her.

"I've gone out at five forty-five sharp every day since I've been here. Allen can attest to that."

Valerie chimed in. "Have you caught anything?"

Dempsey glared at her. "I haven't been very lucky this trip, but I got a deer on Sunday morning. It's in the chiller now. You can ask Allen if you don't believe me."

"I will ask him," Charlene told him. "Did you have any relationship with Porteus Patterson?"

"He was my brother-in-law," Dempsey replied.

Charlene gasped. "You're his brother-in-law? Did you come up here to hunt together?"

"Hunt?" Dempsey barked. "Porteus never hunted in his life."

"What I mean is," Charlene explained, "did you come up here to meet him?"

"I didn't know he was going to be here when I booked the trip," Dempsey replied. "I was as surprised as anybody to find him here."

"Do you know what Porteus was doing up here?" Charlene asked.

"I have no idea," Dempsey replied.

Charlene sighed. "Well, we're not getting anywhere, are we? What about you, Andrea? What were you doing up here?"

Andrea grumbled under her breath. "Nothing."

Charlene stared at her. "You must have been doing something. Did you come up here to hunt?"

"I'm not doing anything up here," Andrea shot back. "I'm sitting around doing nothing."

Valerie and Charlene looked at each other. Charlene took a deep breath. "I understand you probably don't want to answer questions about your personal life. But a man is dead under suspicious circumstances, and if there was any foul play involved, one of the people at this Lodge must be responsible. We might not be the local police, but we're law enforcement officers nonetheless. You're all under the same obligation to cooperate with our investigation as you would be with the police."

Silence answered her. Heinrich gazed out toward the pool, and Dempsey fiddled with his fingers in his lap. Only Andrea looked directly into their eyes. "You won't find any of your answers here."

"You can't withhold material evidence from this investigation," Charlene told her.

"We don't have to withhold evidence," Andrea replied. "We don't have any evidence to withhold because none of us had anything to do with Porteus Patterson's death. The maintenance man killed him. Why don't you investigate him and leave us alone?"

Chapter 4

Charlene strode down the hall, and Valerie stumbled over her own feet to keep up with her.

"What did you think of all that?"

"They're hiding something," Valerie panted. "They know something and they're not telling."

"That's what I think, too," Charlene replied.

"How could an economist be Member at Large for the Veterinarian's Professional Society?" Valerie asked.

"And that Dempsey Doolittle never went hunting on the back of any horse. I doubt he could walk out to the stables, let alone ride into the mountains to hunt deer."

Charlene grinned at her. "Anything else that stuck out at you?"

"Andrea," Valerie replied.

"What about her?" Charlene asked.

"Everything about her," Valerie replied. "Everything about her stuck out at me. Okay, so Dempsey and Heinrich lied about what they were doing here, but Andrea didn't even try." Valerie paused a moment to consider.

"She said she wasn't doing anything up here, but that's not possible. She must have come up here for something, even if was just a little R and R. She didn't just drop out of the sky."

"Good work," Charlene told her.

"And what about Allen?" Valerie asked. "He sure was quick to pin the blame on Jeff when he had a key to the power station in his office all along."

Charlene stopped walking and rounded on Valerie. "What did you say?"

"I said," Valerie repeated, "Allen was quick to pin the blame on Jeff when he had a key to the power station in his office."

Charlene narrowed her eyes. "You better clean up your act, Valerie, or you won't be my partner for long. I don't know how to warn you about this other than to say I won't stand for it."

Valerie gasped. "What are you talking about?"

"You're besotted with that maintenance man," Charlene shot back. "It's written all over your face. I don't know how it could have happened so fast, because you only just laid eyes on him a minute ago and now you're head over heels over him."

"I am not," Valerie insisted.

"You just called him Jeff," Charlene pointed out. "You don't even know him, and you're calling him by his first name."

Valerie's cheeks burned, but she had to hold Charlene's gaze. She couldn't back down now without admitting her guilt. "That doesn't mean I'm besotted with him."

Charlene gritted her teeth. "We're on our way to interview him right now, so do yourself, and me, a big favor. Don't say a word. Let me do the interviewing, and you just stand there and observe."

A lump stuck in Valerie's throat. "Is that really necessary? I thought you said I was doing good."

"That was before," Charlene replied. "I wouldn't mind you putting your two cents into the interview if I could trust you to behave."

"You can trust me to behave, Charlene," Valerie told her. "I won't do anything out of line during the interview."

Charlene let out a deep breath. "It's still your first day. Let me take the lead on this one. If everything goes smoothly, we'll reconsider later."

Valerie started to protest, but the expression on Charlene's face changed her mind. "All right."

They continued walking to the end of the corridor, where Charlene let them out onto the grounds through the staff service door. They walked on through the gardens to a wooden shed tucked into the trees. Jeff Everson waited for them at the door.

Charlene strode right up to him and stuck out her hand. "Thanks for meeting with us, Jeff. I'm Charlene Brockworth. I'm a federal investigator looking into Porteus Patterson's death."

"I know who you are," Jeff replied. "Everybody knows who you are, Charlene."

Charlene started back in surprise. "Most people who know me are law enforcement officers. How do you know who I am?"

"I know all about you and the Strikeforce Investigation Team," Jeff replied. "I may not be a law enforcement officer, but I wasn't born under a rock."

Charlene looked around the grounds. "You've been working here for the last five years, so you might as well have been."

"I wasn't born here," Jeff replied. "I keep up with business on the outside. We have the internet up here, you know."

Charlene studied him. "What can you tell us about Patterson's death?"

"Nothing Allen hasn't already told you," Jeff replied. "I found Patterson dead in the power station room. The door was locked from the outside, and since I'm the only one with a key — besides him, of course — Allen decided I must have killed him. But I didn't, and Allen knows that as well as I do."

Charlene nodded. "Did you have any connection with Patterson before that?"

"None at all," Jeff replied. "I met him the few times he came up here, but that's all. It's the other guests who have a connection with him. You should ask them about that."

"I know Dempsey Doolittle was Patterson's brother-in-law," Charlene told him. "I don't know about the others."

"They all have a connection with him, not just Dempsey," Jeff countered. "They all came up here to meet."

Charlene studied him. "What did they come up here to meet about?"

"I have no idea," Jeff replied. "But they've spent all their time together since they got here. It's like that every time they come. They meet on the deck every morning after breakfast, and I've seen them with their heads together just about every other time, too."

"You can't be serious," Charlene exclaimed. "They have nothing to do with each other. Heinrich Wiesenthal was attending a conference in Denver for the Veterinarians' Professional Society, and Dempsey came up for the hunting...."

Jeff shook his head. "Maybe that's the story they spun for you, but it's a front for what they're really doing. They came here to meet. I'm telling you."

"Who exactly came here to meet?" Charlene asked. "Was it Patterson and Dempsey and Heinrich, or just Patterson and Dempsey? Who?"

"All of them," Jeff shot back. "Patterson, Dempsey, Heinrich, and that Swain lady. They've been together every minute of the day, and I wouldn't be surprised if they met at night, too."

Valerie couldn't keep quiet any longer. "What about Babette Cooney? Did she meet with them, too?"

Charlene scowled at her, but Jeff didn't notice. "No, she wasn't involved. I didn't see her anywhere near the other guests."

Charlene glanced at Valerie, then went back to questioning Jeff.

"What do you know about them? What do you know about each of the guests you just mentioned?"

"All I know about them," Jeff replied, "is that they've all got a lot more money than I have. I know that Swain woman...."

"Her name's Andrea," Charlene interrupted. "You can call her by her name."

"Fine. Andrea," Jeff went on. "I know she's some kind of heiress. And I know Dempsey is some kind of political consultant. I guess Heinrich is a vet."

Charlene's head whipped around. "What makes you say that?"

"You just said he was attending the conference of the Veterinarians' Professional Society," Jeff replied. "He wouldn't be attending that if he wasn't a vet, would he?"

Charlene snorted. "Never mind about that. So you saw the guests meeting, and you claim you know nothing about Patterson's death."

"I don't," he replied.

"That's what everybody says," Charlene grumbled. "When this is all over, I'm going to arrest somebody for obstruction of justice."

"It won't be me," Jeff replied. "I've told you everything I know."

Charlene nodded. "Thank you for telling us. It gives us something to go on, anyway."

Jeff glanced at Valerie. "Are you sure there's nothing more you want to ask me?"

Charlene started to say, "No," when Valerie stepped forward. Her words came out in a rush, but she just had to find out who he was before Charlene cut her off.

"You've been working here for five years. What did you do before that?"

Charlene grabbed Valerie's jacket by the sleeve and yanked her back. "What did I tell you?"

Jeff didn't pay any attention. He kept his gaze fixed on Valerie.

"I worked at a hotel in Denver."

"And before that?" Valerie asked. "You might not be a law enforcement officer, but I'll bet you have some kind of paramilitary training. Am I wrong?"

Jeff smiled and shook his head. "I went through Navy SEAL training. I served a tour of duty in Mombasa, but that's all. I decided I wanted a quiet life in the mountains instead."

Valerie nodded. "Thanks. That's what I thought."

Charlene spun around on her heel and stomped away through the bushes. With one last smile to Jeff, Valerie hurried after her. At the service door, Charlene rounded on Valerie with her teeth bared.

"You can't even follow simple instructions to stay out of an interview with a murder suspect. What is wrong with you? I ought to pack you off to the Alleycat Boarding House right now."

"Come on, Charlene," Valerie returned.

"You have to admit Jeff couldn't have killed Patterson. He's an ex-Navy SEAL. He's practically one of us. He's probably the one person in this whole kooky Lodge that's telling the truth. You heard what he said. The guests came up here to meet. They weren't attending conferences or hunting or anything else. Porteus Patterson was a major shipping magnate, and these people came up here to meet with him in private. They've got something going on that they don't want us to know about."

Charlene clenched her jaw. "You can't take his word over theirs. You have no proof that he's telling the truth. He could have concocted the whole thing to divert suspicion from himself and cast it onto them."

Valerie shook her head. "You know as well as I do he wouldn't do that. You must have been able to detect the lies in their stories. He wasn't lying. He couldn't lie about something like that."

"How do you know he wasn't trained to lie?" Charlene shot back. "He could be an operative sent here to bump off Patterson. He's got the paramilitary training to do it."

Valerie shook her head. "He wouldn't still be hanging around here for us to interview if he was. He would be halfway to Siberia by now."

Charlene's shoulders slumped in defeat. "All right. I'm willing to go along with this for the time being. Let's do some more digging, and we can see if your friend Jeff is telling the truth. If he is, and the guests met here for some secret reason, one of them might have had a motive to kill Patterson."

"If he's telling the truth," Valerie pointed out, "he could help us with the investigation. He could have more useful information about the guests and their activities."

Charlene stiffened. "Don't push it. He's still a suspect, and we have to treat him as one."

Chapter 5

Valerie kicked off her shoes and sat cross-legged on Charlene's bed. She settled her computer on her lap and opened her web browser. Charlene sat at the table across the room and worked on her laptop.

"Well, the guests seem to check out. Andrea's record is squeaky clean. She's never even had a parking ticket in her life."

"Maybe she doesn't know how to drive," Valerie suggested.

Charlene chuckled. "Heinrich really is an economist based in Montreal, and he really is Member at Large of the Veterinarians' Professional Society, which just concluded its annual conference in Denver. He was telling the truth about that. And Dempsey has been coming to the Mackenzie Lodge every year at this time, and he's bought a hunting license every year, too. So we've got nothing on any of them."

"Unfortunately," Valerie countered, "I can't say the same for our friend Porteus Patterson. I just looked him up in the federal database, and he's got a file the size of Detroit. He's been under investigation by the FBI a dozen times for money laundering, drug running, and customs violations with his shipping business." Valerie looked a bit grim as she spoke.

"Every time they get close to nailing him, he runs home to Canada, so the case has to be transferred to the CIA. Then when the CIA gets close to nailing him, he moves back to the States. He's played the two agencies against each other for decades, and he always gets away in the end."

"Well, he didn't get away this time, did he?" Charlene replied.

"Maybe he came up here to transact some of his illicit business," Valerie suggested. "Maybe these other guests are involved with it somehow, and this is where they meet to work out their conspiracies."

Charlene laughed out loud. "You're really grasping at straws now. I just told you none of the others has any criminal record."

"Who better to recruit for the job?" Valerie countered. "Don't forget the Mackenzie Lodge is one of the most exclusive, private resorts in the Northern Hemisphere. If clean people with no record wanted to meet an old saw like Porteus Patterson, they couldn't pick a better place to do it. No one would know they ever had any connection with him. We wouldn't know about it ourselves if Patterson hadn't wound up dead."

"If they came up here to do business with him, and wanted to keep their meeting secret," Charlene asked, "why would they kill him? That would only attract attention to themselves and the very activities they wanted to hide."

"Maybe they counted on sticking the blame on Jeff," Valerie suggested.

"Maybe they wanted to get rid of Patterson, so they did it in a way that would cover up the fact that they came here to meet with him."

Charlene shook her head. "You've got to stop calling him Jeff."

Valerie's head shot up. "What should I call him instead—Mr. Everson?"

"I don't care what you call him as long as it isn't Jeff," Charlene replied. "You're investigating a death here. You can't get on familiar terms with someone you might wind up arresting."

Valerie sighed. This whole Jeff thing was getting out of hand.

"All right."

Charlene closed her laptop. "Let's go check out the guests' stories. We'll start with Dempsey. He claims he brought in a deer. We can verify that, at least."

The two women wandered around the Lodge for almost an hour before they stopped in front of the reception desk. Allen's tepid smile evaporated when he saw the investigators. "Can I help you?"

"Where do you keep your chiller?" Charlene asked.

"My what?" Allen asked.

"Your chiller," Charlene repeated.

"Where do your guests store the meat they bring in after their hunting trips."

Allen waved his hand over his shoulder. "It's behind the kitchen near the walk-in freezer."

"We want to look at it," Charlene told him.

Allen froze. "What for? What does that have to do with Mr. Patterson's death?"

"Dempsey Doolittle claims he brought in a deer and stored the carcass in your chiller," Charlene replied. "We want to verify it's there."

Allen's eyes shifted right, then left. "Mr. Doolittle didn't bring in any deer. The only deer in the chiller belongs to Mr. Patterson."

Charlene looked at Valerie. "But Mr. Doolittle told us Mr. Patterson didn't hunt. He said he never hunted in his life. Why would he lie about that?"

"I'm sorry," Allen replied, "but Mr. Doolittle knows very well that Mr. Patterson did hunt. They went out together the morning Mr. Patterson died."

Charlene straightened up. "He did?"

Allen nodded. "That was the morning Mr. Patterson brought in the deer. He and Mr. Doolittle went together."

Valerie spoke up. "Did they go on horseback?"

"Horseback!" Allen shrieked. "Of course they didn't go on horseback. What kind of a question is that?"

"Dempsey Doolittle told us he hunts on horseback," Charlene told him.

Allen made a disgusted face.

"Dempsey Doolittle doesn't hunt at all, on horseback or any other way. He never has."

"But you just said he and Mr. Patterson went out together the morning he died," Charlene pointed out. "Which is it?"

"Mr. Patterson hunted," Allen explained, "and Mr. Doolittle went with him that morning. But Mr. Doolittle didn't hunt. He never has. And he never rode any horse." He dissolved into hysterical giggling. "My goodness! Can you imagine a man like that on the back of a horse? He would break the poor creature's legs."

Charlene and Valerie shared a smile.

Allen pulled himself together. "Besides, we don't have hunts on horseback here."

"But you have stables," Valerie pointed out.

"Those horses are for pleasure riding, not hunting," Allen replied. "They aren't trained to stand still during gunfire. They're for pleasure riding in the dressage ring or on short rides around the Lodge. We don't recommend riding to hunt."

"But Dempsey Doolittle bought a hunting license every year when he came up here," Charlene pointed out. "Why would he do that if he didn't intend to hunt?"

Allen held up both hands. "I couldn't speak to Mr. Dempsey's motives. You'll have to ask him that."

"I will." Charlene took a step forward. "Show us this chiller. I want to see the carcass."

"Follow me." Allen led them through the steamy kitchen. The chefs and dishwashers glanced up as they passed.

They passed through the back door to a dirty yard with two identical steel shipping containers on either side. A dense hedge clipped to form a solid wall of green separated the yard from the rest of the grounds.

Valerie looked over her shoulder at the Lodge. None of the guest windows looked out on this part of the property. None of the guests would ever have known the yard was there. Only one balcony extended over the hedge and looked out toward the mountains.

Allen pulled open the door of one of the containers. "Here you go. Here's the chiller."

A gust of freezing cold air blasted into Valerie's face. She wrapped her arms around her chest, and she and Charlene peered into the frosty gloom. A long, lean form of bare red meat hung from the ceiling. Steel shelves lined either side, and bundles wrapped in white paper and plastic cluttered the shelves.

Charlene's teeth chattered. "Is that the only carcass you have?"

"That's what I told you," Allen replied. "Mr. Patterson is the only guest we have right now who hunts—I mean, he hunted. He doesn't anymore, for obvious reasons."

"What will you do with the carcass?" Valerie asked.

Allen closed the door and fitted the latch in place. "We'll use it in the kitchen. I don't expect Mr. Patterson's relatives to claim it."

Valerie turned away. "No, I suppose they won't."

"It happens all the time," Allen remarked.

Valerie's head whipped around. "What does? Your guests turning up dead?"

Allen twittered with laughter. "No, my dear lady, no, they don't turn up dead. They leave their kills behind. They go out hunting for the sport of it. The Lodge provides a processing service to bring the meat in, and the guests want to have some of it for dinner. But after that, they often forget all about it. They neglect to arrange to transport the meat home with them, and they leave it here. We label it for thirty days, and then we use it in the kitchen for our other guests."

Charlene surveyed the yard. "That's pretty good for you. You must save a lot of money on food cost."

Allen shrugged. "Not so much."

They followed him back to the reception area. "Thank you, Allen."

He bowed, and his tranquil smile returned. "You lovely ladies must let me know if there is anything else I can do for you."

"Do you happen to know if Mr. Patterson met with any of the other guests during his stay?" Charlene asked.

Allen threw back his shoulders. "He didn't meet with them. He didn't even know them."

"Except for Mr. Doolittle, you mean," Valerie corrected.

Allen flapped both hands from the wrists. "You know what I mean."

"No, we don't know what you mean," Charlene replied. "Mr. Patterson met with Mr. Doolittle to go hunting. Maybe he met with him at other times, too. Maybe he talked to the other guests on the deck in the morning after breakfast. Is that possible?"

"Of course he met with Mr. Doolittle," Allen shot back. "They're brothers-in-law. It would be unheard of if they didn't see each other during their stay."

"And the others?" Charlene asked.

"Of course he talked to them on the deck after breakfast," Allen screeched. "All the guests go out to the deck after breakfast. What else is there for them to do?"

"What about other times?" Charlene asked. "Did they get together at other times?"

"I'm sure I don't know," Allen snapped. "I don't keep track of my guests' activities."

"But you must keep a record of who checked out swimming towels for the pool." Valerie ticked the items off on her fingers. "And who got the billiard balls for the games room, and who took the horses riding at the dressage ring. You must have some information about your guests' activities."

Allen stared at her. "What are you accusing me of?"

"I'm not accusing you of anything," Valerie replied. "I'm just saying you're being awfully protective of your guests' information. A businessman like you ought to cooperate as fully as possible with this investigation."

He opened his mouth, but no sound came out. Valerie smiled at him.

Charlene stepped in. "Listen, Allen. I understand you want to protect your guests' privacy, but you're under suspicion for Patterson's death, too, you know. If you know what's good for you, you should give us all the information you have on your guests."

Allen stared at them. Then his lip quivered. All at once, he covered his face with his hands and burst into tears. He ran away from them back into his office.

Charlene and Valerie stared after him. Then they looked at each other. They waited, but Allen didn't come back. They looked at each other again. Charlene blinked. "Was it something I said?"

Valerie turned away. "I'm hungry. I'm going to the dining room to get a sandwich. Do you want anything?"

"I'm not hungry," Charlene replied. "I'll go look around and meet you back at my room to go over what we have so far. Then we'll take another crack at the guests. We'll confront them about the lies they told us."

"Only Dempsey Doolittle lied," Valerie pointed out. "We don't have anything to confront the others about."

"We can ask them about meeting Patterson," Charlene replied.

"Like Allen said," Valerie argued, "that could have been perfectly innocent."

Charlene shrugged. "Maybe, but I don't think so."

"So," Valerie asked, "are you starting to believe what Je....I mean, the maintenance man.... said about the guests meeting each other during their stay?"

Charlene turned away.

"I don't know what to believe. Go get your sandwich and meet me back at my room."

"All right," Valerie replied. "I'll see you later."

Chapter 6

Valerie picked up a roast beef sandwich from the dining room, but she didn't feel like eating it there. She didn't feel like taking it back to Charlene's room, either. She wanted to have a good poke around, too. So she strolled back down the hall to the deck. The other guests were gone, so she sat down under the umbrella to eat. The sun glinted off the pool and blinded her. She fought back the urge to drift off to sleep.

All of a sudden, she snapped alert when she spotted Jeff Everson moving through the grounds. Did he see her? She wiped the breadcrumbs off her face and swallowed her mouthful of sandwich. He paused between the bushes and glanced up at her. "Where's your partner?"

"She's back in her room," Valerie replied. "I'm supposed to meet her as soon as I finish eating."

"Why don't you come down here and take a walk with me?" Jeff suggested.

Valerie shivered and glanced around. No one would see her if she went with him "I couldn't do that. I'm supposed to be investigating you in connection with Patterson's death. Why don't you come up here and sit down at the table under the umbrella instead?"

Jeff grinned and shook his head. "I'm not allowed to. This is one of the guest areas, and I'm not allowed to enter the guest areas. I'm supposed to stay out here in the grounds. If you want to talk to me, you'll have to come down here."

"Are you allowed to talk to the guests?" she asked.

He inclined his head to one side. "You're not a guest, are you? You're an investigator."

"That's true," she replied. "That's all the more reason why I shouldn't be talking to you at all."

"Then you'll just have to whisper to me through the bushes," he told her.

That was too much for Valerie. She scooped up the rest of her sandwich and descended the steps. His smile widened when she met him between the shrubs. "That's more like it. Now we can talk like civilized human beings."

Valerie took another bite of her sandwich. "Thanks again for telling us about Patterson meeting the other guests. That was a big help."

He studied her. "You did well to find out about my background. You're the first person in almost ten years who has asked enough of the right kinds of questions to find out."

"I'm sure Charlene would have found out sooner or later," Valerie told him. "She's a legend in the law enforcement community, and she's the first woman to be selected to the Strikeforce Team."

"I know that," he replied, "but she didn't ask, did she? You did."

Valerie blushed. "I wanted to know about you. I could tell the first time I saw you that you weren't any ordinary maintenance man. I knew you were some kind of military or law enforcement."

"What gave it away?" he asked.

Valerie studied him. "It must have been something in your eyes."

He didn't laugh the way she thought he would. He locked his eyes on hers, and she fell headlong into the deep pools of his gaze. "Where have you been all my life?"

Valerie shifted from one foot to the other. "I haven't been anywhere. You've been hiding up here in the mountains."

He let out his breath, and his nostrils flared.

"Charlene thinks you might be some kind of operative," Valerie went on. "She thinks you were planted here to bump off Patterson."

"What do you think about that?" he asked.

"I think if that was the case," Valerie replied, "you would have disappeared as soon as Patterson stopped breathing. We wouldn't be talking now if you were."

"So who do you think killed Patterson?" he asked.

"Maybe nobody killed him," Valerie replied. "Maybe he met someone at the power station, or planned to meet someone there, and fell and hit his head. Maybe he stumbled into a live circuit and electrocuted himself. Maybe he attacked the person he was meeting and they killed him in self-defense. We really don't know."

Jeff nodded. "So what are you going to do about it?"

Valerie swallowed her sandwich. "Charlene doesn't want me talking to you, but I was thinking. You see and hear things around this place no one else sees and hears. You're also the only person here I'm certain is innocent. Don't ask me how I know it, because if Charlene finds out about this, I'm out of a job."

Jeff's eyes widened. "We don't want that. You don't want to get kicked off the Strikeforce Team."

"Especially not since today is my very first day," Valerie added. "I never would have dreamed I'd be Charlene Brockworth's partner, but I am, and I don't want to jeopardize that."

"And yet," he countered, "here you are, talking to me."

"That's because I think you can help us," Valerie told him. "You can keep an eye on the guests for us. You can tell us what they're up to and who's meeting who and when. I don't trust anyone else to do that for us."

"What about Allen?" he asked.

Valerie shook her head. "He's a suspect, too. He had the only other key to the power station. He could have used it to kill Patterson, or he could have given it to the person who did."

"Why would he do that?" Jeff asked. "What motive could he have?"

"What motive could any of them have?" Valerie argued. "Patterson had a history of illegal activity, and you said he met with the others. They could have been working for him, and Allen could have been doing the same thing."

Jeff shrugged. "I've known Allen a long time. He doesn't have the brains or the backbone to do anything illegal."

"Not even if a mastermind like Patterson told him what to do?" Valerie asked.

"I doubt it," Jeff replied. "I would be very surprised if he did."

"Then how do you explain the power station being locked from the outside?" Valerie asked. "Someone unlocked the door, took Patterson in there, and then locked the door again after he was dead."

"Have you seen the power station?" Jeff asked.

Valerie fidgeted. "No, I haven't. But I'm sure Charlene will want to examine the scene pretty soon."

Jeff jerked his head over his shoulder. "Why don't you come with me and have a look at it now?"

Valerie glanced back toward the Lodge. What if Charlene found out she was sneaking around with Jeff behind her back? Then she noticed Jeff watching her and she cast all caution to the wind. "Oh, all right."

He led her around the building where a concrete bunker jutted out of the foundation. A solid iron door blocked the entrance to the power station. Jeff went right up to it, planted his hand on the door, and pushed it open.

Valerie cried out in surprise. "But it isn't even locked. Why haven't they kept the door locked?"

Jeff stood back. "Take a look."

Valerie peered into the gloom. Then she spied something metallic sticking out of the edge of the door. A massive dial stuck out of the door.

"It's a timer lock," Jeff told her. "The door locks and unlocks at certain times of the day. The key overrides the lock, but when the door is unlocked, anyone can open it. No one had to lock Patterson in here. He could have walked in on his own, as long as he came during the hours of ten in the morning and two in the afternoon."

"Why those hours?" Valerie asked. "Why is it unlocked then?"

"This used to be an old hospital building," Jeff explained. "Allen converted it into a hunting lodge. This used to be an old store room, and the door was unlocked from ten to two to let the supply matron get supplies during those hours. Allen never changed the door."

Valerie shook her head. "Then Patterson's death could have been an accident. He could have come in here by himself and accidentally electrocuted."

"Not necessarily." He took a flashlight out of his pocket and pointed it into the room. "Take a closer look."

Valerie crept into the room. Dials and electrical panels covered the far wall, but in front of them, iron bars blocked them off from the rest of the room. No one could accidentally fall into that. Valerie nodded. "Now I see."

Jeff came to her side.

"Where did you find his body?" she asked.

"Over here." He moved away into the shadows.

Valerie followed him to a corner where the light coming through the door couldn't penetrate. A corner of the wall jutted out into the room and formed a narrow alley away from the power panels. Two solid concrete walls rose from either side. Jeff trained his flashlight beam into the corner. "He was right here."

Valerie looked around her. "How could he be electrocuted way over here?"

"He could have been dragged here," Jeff pointed out. "He could have been killed somewhere else and hidden here."

Valerie turned away. The flashlight gave Jeff a ghostly appearance. "How often did you come in here? Did you have a regular schedule for coming in here?"

"I came every morning at ten when the lock opened," Jeff replied. "I would check all the read-outs to make sure all the circuits were operating normally. Other than that, I only came down here when we had a power outage or a short somewhere in the building."

"So did you find him at your morning check?" Valerie asked.

"No. I came down here to throw the breaker on the pool pump," he replied. "It shorted out, and I had to come here to turn it back on. It was three o'clock in the afternoon."

"What made it blow out?" Valerie asked.

Jeff grinned. "We have frogs living in our pool shed. Every now and again, one of them hops on the power cable going from the main building supply to the pump. They knock the cable loose and short out the pump."

"Are you sure it's the frogs doing it?" Valerie asked.

Jeff chuckled. "I don't think I could mistake the fried frog lying on the ground under the cable."

Valerie nodded. "All right. Let's get out of here. This place gives me the creeps."

Jeff shut the door behind them. "That should satisfy your partner."

"Nothing will satisfy her," Valerie returned. "She'll have to come down here and see everything for herself." Jeff walked her back to the deck. Valerie hesitated. "I better go. Charlene will be wondering where I am."

"Let's do this again some time," he suggested, "some time when we won't be talking about this case."

Valerie tried to tear her eyes away from his face. "I don't know when that will be. As soon as we solve this case, we'll be on our way back to Denver."

"Then let's do it sometime before the case is resolved," Jeff suggested.

"I don't know." Valerie dropped her hands to her side. "I don't like sneaking around on Charlene."

"Then don't sneak around," Jeff told her. "Tell her the truth. Tell her you're coming out to meet me."

Valerie snorted. "She'd have my head in a vise so fast I wouldn't be able to see straight."

"What's the big deal?" Jeff asked.

"She doesn't even like me calling you Jeff," Valerie replied. "She says I'm besotted with someone I might have to arrest for murder."

He fixed his eyes on her face again, and this time, there was no mirth in his expression. "I noticed you the first time I saw you, too. I knew you were ten times the investigator Charlene is."

Valerie kicked at a clump of grass at her feet. "I should get going."

He caught hold of her hand and held her back. "I'll let you go right now, Valerie, but I won't let you go forever. I've never met anyone like you before, and I won't let you slip out of my life. I've been living alone up here for five years. I didn't realize how much I needed someone like you."

Valerie pulled her hand out of his grasp. "Don't start talking like that. We just met."

But he wouldn't let her pull away. He towered over her, and his form blocked out her view of everything else. Her breath rasped in and out of her lungs. She tried again to pull her hand out of his grip, but before she could do anything, he moved in and kissed her. She really stopped breathing then, but she was too surprised to stop him. In an instant, his warm lips hypnotized her and she couldn't have pulled away even if she wanted to. She melted into his kiss, and his arms folded around her. He crushed the rest of the air out her lungs, and all her resistance vanished. Her body sagged into his embrace.

He understood better than Valerie did herself what that meant, and his lips pressed down harder than ever on her mouth.

Her mouth opened and a faint moan escaped her. What was happening? She couldn't convince her mind to function.

A hot streak of passionate desire crackled along her nerves. How long had it been since a man fired her this way? She couldn't hold back from him. She wouldn't even try. She let her mouth open to his.

A breeze fanned her fevered cheeks. Jeff brought himself out of the bubble of their isolated intimacy first, and he guided her backwards. Back toward the bushes. At least one of them was still thinking clearly.

Then, with startling suddenness, Valerie snapped alert. If he got her behind those bushes, no one would be able to see them together. They could do whatever they wanted, and no one would know. Jeff could do whatever he wanted and no one would know.

She couldn't let that happen. She'd just met him a few hours ago, and he was a suspect in a murder she was supposed to be investigating. She couldn't stagger off into the bushes with him — not until she proved for certain that he was innocent.

With an almighty effort, she tore herself out of his arms. But she couldn't stand around to deal with his reaction. She couldn't trust herself even to look into his face without falling under his spell again. She ran for the deck and took the steps two at a time.

By the time she turned around he had already vanished into the bushes.

Chapter 7

Valerie raced along the hall back to Charlene's room. She couldn't let Charlene find out what had just happened. What a fool she was to get started with Jeff like that when he could be the killer they'd come up here to catch. She would have to guard herself against him from now on.

She burst into the room all out of breath, but when she looked around, she found it empty. Charlene's laptop sat open on the desk, but Charlene herself was nowhere in sight. Valerie choked back her breath and set her own computer out on the table.

She'd settled down to review the case, and look up some more information on the principle characters, when she heard noise coming from the bathroom. She ignored it for a while, but it didn't go away. After another period of trying unsuccessfully to block out the sound, she started to feel uneasy and went to see what it was.

She shoved the bathroom door open and found the room full of steam. It billowed out of the shower stall and fogged the mirror. Valerie waved it aside. "I'm back, Charlene. As soon as you get out of the shower, I've got something to show you."

No one answered. Valerie listened.

The shower noise that disturbed her work made a steady rain against the shower wall. None of the splashes or sloshes of normal shower sounds came out of the stall.

"Are you there, Charlene?"

Still nothing. Valerie took another step into the bathroom and, with her breath sticking in her throat, she peeked around the corner of the stall. The shower was empty.

Valerie gasped out loud. Where was Charlene? She flipped the handle down, and the shower died.

Valerie whirled around and raced out to the main room. She dashed over to Charlene's computer, punched in the code Charlene had given her, and pulled up the last page Charlene had been looking at. It was a document from the federal database related to Jeff Everson's service in Africa. She scrolled down and found a list of citations a mile long, including the Navy Cross for service above and beyond the call of duty.

Valerie snapped the laptop closed. Jeff couldn't be a killer. She just knew it. He was too good, too helpful. She strode out of the room and down the hall. She had to find Charlene. She passed the big windows overlooking the deck and pool. Dempsey Doolittle's gargantuan form stuck out from under the umbrella. Were the other guests with him? Were they meeting to discuss their nefarious conspiracies again?

Maybe she'd just made up all that nonsense about conspiracies. Maybe Jeff saw the guests together in complete innocence. Maybe they met on the deck every morning after breakfast as a matter of habit, not to plot the overthrow of the civilized world.

She moved farther down the hall and took another look. Yes, there they were. The Three Musketeers. Dempsey, Heinrich, and Andrea, together forever. One for all and all for one. What were they up to? They must be very intimate to spend all their time together. No one came up to a remote mountain hunting lodge to spend that kind of time with strangers.

Andrea glanced up at the window and noticed Valerie watching them. Valerie hurried away and found her way back to the reception desk. Allen glanced up from his computer screen when she appeared. "Yes?"

"Have you seen my partner, Allen?" she asked. "I just went to her room and found her computer up and running and the shower on, but she's not there."

"I'm sure she's somewhere around the Lodge," Allen replied. "Have you checked the library?"

Valerie narrowed her eyes. "Charlene's a seasoned federal agent. She wouldn't just walk out of her room like that. Have you seen her at all?"

Allen sniffed. "No, I haven't. I don't keep track of my guests the way you seem to think I do."

"I only thought...." Valerie began.

Allen cut her off with a wave of his hand. "I know what you thought. You thought I kept a record of my guests' comings and goings, when they check out the swimming towels and when they get the billiard balls for the games room. I know what you thought."

"Allen...." Valerie stammered.

He chopped the air with his hand. "Don't come crying to me now you've lost your partner. I run an exclusive lodge here. If people don't want every Tom, Dick, and Harry poking their noses into their business, it's my job to make sure their privacy is respected. Are you capable of understanding that?"

Valerie stiffened. Rising alarm scorched through her chest, and she fought back the urge to grab him by the shirt collar and give him a good hard shake. "Listen, Allen. We aren't talking about your exclusive guests. We're talking about a federal agent who came up here to investigate a suspicious death — a death, I might add, for which you yourself are under suspicion. Now that agent has disappeared under the most sudden and mysterious circumstances. The least you can do is help me find her."

Allen glared at her. Then he wilted. "She hasn't disappeared. She must be somewhere around the Lodge. Take a look around, and I'm sure you'll find her."

Valerie pursed her lips and stalked off. She wouldn't forget his stubborn attitude. She would find a way to pay him back for his superiority when this case was all settled. In the meantime, though, she had to find Charlene. She went back along the hall to the dining room, then to the library and the games room. Charlene was nowhere to be found.

She left word at each place for Charlene to find her as soon as possible, but none of the staff or guests had seen Charlene. None of them could fail to match her with Valerie's description of a tall woman with flaming red hair, jeans, and snakeskin cowboy boots.

Valerie hurried back to the service door and out into the grounds. She gasped for breath, but she swallowed her rising panic and commanded her mind to think. Where could Charlene be at a time like this? Valerie raced down to the stables, but found only the stable boys. They gave her curious looks, but they couldn't help her.

She set off at a dead run back to the Lodge. What would she do if she couldn't find Charlene? Was Charlene in danger? Did she ditch her? How could she take over this case alone? Her mind was spinning with questions, concern and fear. She tried to shove all but finding Charlene out of her mind, but when she rounded the camellia bushes, she collided with Jeff coming the other way. She bounced off his chest.

"Hey, where's the fire?"

Valerie stared up into his face. "Jeff, I was just...."

He held her by the shoulders at arm's length. "Were you looking for me? Is there anything I can do for you?"

"I was looking for Charlene," Valerie replied. "She's gone."

He raised his eyebrows. "What do you mean, gone?"

"Just.... gone," Valerie stammered. "After I left you, I went back to her room. We were supposed to meet there after I got something to eat. I found her computer turned on. She was looking up your military service record. And the shower was on but she wasn't there. Now I can't find her."

Jeff clenched his teeth. He seized Valerie's hand.

"Come on. I'll help you find her." He set off toward the Lodge.

Valerie held him back. "Wait, Jeff. You can't go up there like this. You'll get in trouble, and I'm not sure if Charlene really is missing. She could have gone off somewhere to have a look around. I might find her in a minute or two."

Jeff eyed her. "Do you really believe that?"

Valerie dropped her eyes to the ground. "No, I am worried. What if she's in trouble? She's tough but this is weird. If she's really missing, it is clearly still dangerous here... and, it means I'm in charge of this investigation."

"That's right," Jeff replied. "Do you want to call for back-up?"

"Not yet," Valerie replied. "Charlene could turn up again at any time, but if I'm taking charge of the investigation, I'd better get to work."

"I'll help you," Jeff told her. "You don't have to do this alone."

Valerie drew back. "No. Charlene was right. I have to keep my distance from you. As long as you're involved in this case, I can't let my feelings for you cloud my investigation."

He frowned, but then his face softened. "There. You said it."

"What?" she asked.

"You said you have feelings for me," he repeated.

Valerie's shoulders relaxed. "You know I do."

He let her go. "That's all that matters."

Valerie raced away up the steps and into the Lodge. She was headed back toward the reception desk when she spotted Andrea going into the dining room. Dempsey and Heinrich walked side by side right behind her. Valerie narrowed her eyes at them, but Andrea paused on the threshold and glared at her with such a withering expression that Valerie caved and looked away first. When she looked back, the party was gone.

Allen wasn't behind the reception desk. What could she do next to find Charlene? She couldn't keep racing around the lodge like a chicken with her head cut off. She had to think, to work this out systematically. She made up her mind to go back to Charlene's room and wait for her. If she didn't come back by dinner time, she would declare her partner missing.

Declare her partner missing! Nothing in all her training had prepared her for this possibility. None of her instructors or superiors had ever mentioned it. Every law enforcement officer she knew took it as a given that they would have a partner by their side in every case. Law enforcement officers weren't supposed to work alone.

What if Charlene was dead? What if Valerie lost her partner on her first day of work? What would happen to her cherished dream of working on the Strikeforce Team? Valerie shuddered at her confused, competing thoughts.

Back in Charlene's room, Valerie slammed the door and sat down in front of the computer. She couldn't think about Charlene right now. She'd done everything possible to find her, and if Charlene was alive somewhere on the property, she would come back to this room before the night was out.

If she wasn't alive, or if she was in trouble for any reason, the answer to her whereabouts lay in the case of Porteus Patterson's death. Valerie would concentrate on that while she waited. She trawled through all the records. Her email dinged announcing an incoming message. The Coroner's Report was finished and attached. She opened the file on Patterson and almost died of shock.

Porteus Patterson didn't die of electrocution at all. He died from suffocation, with no sign of struggle or blunt force trauma. Since he was found in the power station room, Charlene, and everyone else, had assumed he was electrocuted - and never bothered to check.

So she was right. No one could electrocute themselves in that power room. The iron bars protected the power panels from even the most suicidal visitor.

Thank Heaven for Jeff! If anything happened to Charlene out here in these mountains, at least she had one other ally to rely on. She wasn't completely alone. She would have to ask him about the power station door. The room must be air tight when the door closed and locked at two o'clock. Could Porteus have gone into the room for.... for what? To powder his nose? To straighten his underwear? Whatever the reason, was it possible that he got himself locked in the room and suffocated?

A thousand questions flooded her mind. Who knew, besides Allen and Jeff, that the power room door unlocked automatically every day between ten and two? Who would know that Jeff checked the room every morning to monitor the electrical panels?

Anyone who knew those details would have a perfect opportunity to frame Jeff for murder. She slammed the computer shut and paced the room. Five-thirty came and went. How long should she wait? Charlene could be hurt or dying somewhere on the property. Every minute Valerie waited could cost Charlene her life. She checked the time on the bedside clock every minute and a half. The seconds crept by at an excruciatingly slow pace.

Finally, she stood, and stomped out of the room with Charlene's laptop tucked under her arm. Charlene wasn't coming back. Valerie strode back to the reception desk. She was in charge now, and she would take over this case for better or for worse. She spotted Allen behind the desk and his eyes widened when he saw her coming.

"My dear lady," he began.

She cut him off with a chop of her hand. "You can call me Agent Inglewood, Allen. My partner has disappeared on your property while investigating Porteus Patterson's murder, and I'm taking charge of this case."

Allen gasped. "Murder? What evidence do you have of that?"

Valerie shrugged. "I don't have conclusive evidence that he was murdered, but everything points in that direction. He was suffocated in the power station room. I can only assume he didn't intend to get himself locked in, and now Charlene has disappeared. There's enough suspicious activity going on around here that I'm declaring this a murder investigation. Even if Porteus wasn't murdered, we just might be investigating Charlene's death."

Allen's mouth fell open. "But you don't know....."

Valerie held up her hand to silence him. "You're coming with me to interview the guests. I have some hard questions to ask, and I'm not going to run from one to the next when I could be questioning all of you at once. Now come on."

She spun on her heel and headed back down the hall. He stayed where he was. After she'd gone a few paces, she scowled at him over her shoulder. "If you don't come with me right now, Allen, I'll place you under arrest for Obstruction of Justice."

That made him jump. He scurried around the desk and hurried after her.

Chapter 8

As Valerie expected, the Three Musketeers sat together in the dining room with their dinner plates in front of them. Charlene must be in trouble. She wouldn't miss dinner. Valerie set her jaw and walked right up to their table.

Heinrich smiled at her as she approached. "Ah, Agent.... whatever your name is....."

"Inglewood," Valerie replied. "Agent Inglewood."

"Right. Agent Inglewood," he went on. "So nice to see you again."

"I'm glad you find it nice," Valerie replied. "I'm here to question you all about Porteus's murder."

Dempsey cried out in surprise and almost upset the whole table. Heinrich raised his eyebrows. "So you've determined that it was murder. I thought so."

"Thanks for telling me," Valerie shot back. "I haven't determined it was murder, but I've discovered an overwhelming body of suspicious evidence, so I'm not taking any more chances. One of you killed him. I'm certain of it."

Andrea's languid eyes snapped up to Valerie's face. "What about Allen? He could have killed Porteus."

"I'm here to question him, too," Valerie replied.

"That's why he's here."

Andrea pursed her lips. "So ask your questions."

Valerie set the laptop on the table and opened it. "This is a copy of your last tax return, Andrea."

Andrea scanned the screen. "So what? You won't find anything illegal there. I pay my accountant enough to do the job right."

"I didn't say there was anything illegal," Valerie replied. "Most of your income comes from your father's estate. But you have a laundry list of other, smaller sources of income, too. One of them is an obscure little company by the name of Fidelio Transport out of Dayton, Ohio."

"Did you come all the way down here to tell me that?" Andrea asked. "All that income is legally declared. You can't arrest me for murder on that."

"I didn't say it wasn't legally declared." She turned the computer and changed screens.

"This is your tax return, Heinrich. It follows the same pattern. Most of your income comes from your economic consortium in Montreal, but if you scroll farther down the list of minor income sources, there's the same Fidelio Transport."

Heinrich closed his eyes and smiled. "You're very clever, aren't you?"

"And Dempsey has income from Fidelio Transport, too," Valerie went on.

"The more sources of income you have, the better hidden it is, but it's all there. I'm not surprised Charlene missed it. It could take years for anyone to track the connection between you."

"If that's true," Andrea asked, "why did you discover the connection so quickly? Why didn't it take you years, too?"

"It was Jeff — the maintenance man — who pointed out to me that you three had some closer connection than just sharing a lodge," Valerie told her. "He noticed you three meeting with Porteus on a regular basis, even though you claimed not to have any connection with him — except for Dempsey, of course."

"I don't see what this has to do with his death," Heinrich put in. "So we spent some time with Porteus before his death, and we all have shares in the same company. Big deal. You can't arrest us for that."

"You all have shares in the same company," Valerie corrected. "But Porteus Patterson is listed as Managing Director of Fidelio Transport. The FBI has audited the company five times to try to establish a connection between Fidelio Transport and Porteus's suspicious shipping operations. This Fidelio Transport must be one of his front companies. It seems likely that he's been using it to launder money or bring in illegal goods."

Heinrich looked the other way. Dempsey moved his food around on his plate. Andrea stared straight into Valerie's eyes without blinking.

"If you three hadn't been here at the Lodge at the same time," Valerie went on, "and if Patterson hadn't turned up dead, no one would ever have made the connection between you three, Fidelio Transport and Porteus Patterson."

"You're forgetting one thing, Agent Inglewood," Andrea growled.

"What's that?" Valerie asked.

"If, as you say, we all had shares in one of Porteus's front companies," Andrea replied, "and if, as you say, we all received income from its illegal activity, then none of us would have any reason to kill Porteus. You say no one would have found us out if Porteus hadn't turned up dead. If that's true, none of us would have wanted him dead. Even if one of us did kill him, the guilty party would have left the Lodge as soon as Porteus was dead. The killer wouldn't have stayed around to get caught by you."

Valerie shook her head, but confusion threatened to overwhelm her. "I haven't yet worked out all the details of the case, but at least I know who I'm looking at."

"What about me?" Allen asked. "I wasn't part of this front company."

"You might not have been part of the front company," Valerie explained, "but I'm certain you knew about it. I'm certain you knew Porteus came up here to meet with his three partners in crime. You also knew the power station room would unlock at ten o'clock and re-lock at two o'clock. You would have known the power room was air-tight, and if Porteus wound up locked in there at two o'clock, he would suffocate."

Valerie watched Allen closely as she spoke, delivering the key point last.

"You could be the only person on the property, with the exception of Jeff Everson, who knew that."

Allen fidgeted. "Why would I kill him? Why would I sully the name of my own business by allowing a high profile guest like Mr. Patterson to die on my property?"

"I don't know," Valerie replied. "Maybe you were planted here to kill him. Maybe you got your orders from somewhere else. I can think of half a dozen reasons you would kill him."

Andrea spoke up again. "But you don't have proof of any of this."

"I don't have proof of which of you killed him," Valerie admitted, "but I know for certain now that each of you is a suspect. Each of you lied to me about your connection with him. Heinrich, you and Andrea both told me you didn't have anything to do with Porteus. That was a lie."

"And me?" Dempsey asked. "I didn't lie about my connection with him. I told you he was my brother-in-law."

"But you did lie about going hunting," Valerie pointed out. "You said you brought in a deer, when it was Porteus who did it. You said you went hunting on horseback, which is the biggest joke I've heard all year."

Heinrich snorted with laughter, and even Andrea dropped her eyes to her plate. She chewed her lip to stop herself from laughing. Dempsey puffed out his cheeks. "That doesn't mean I killed him."

"You all must think I'm too stupid to solve this case," Valerie declared. "But I'm going to prove you wrong. When I leave this lodge, I'm taking one of you away with me in handcuffs."

She snapped the laptop closed, whirled away, and stormed out of the dining room. Allen stayed next to the table, and the four of them watched her go. As soon as she got around the corner, she stopped to catch her breath. Her heart thundered in her chest, and her hands trembled around the laptop. She hurried away to her own room. She wouldn't go back to Charlene's room again. She would keep Charlene's laptop with her, even though she had all the same case files and all the same access to the federal database on her own computer.

She couldn't go throwing accusations around without evidence, though. She couldn't confront those people again with nothing to show for it. She had to find some solid evidence of someone's guilt. She had a big pile of wild conjecture topped with circumstantial evidence. She couldn't take anyone away in handcuffs on that.

She rounded the corner toward her room, and the nervous tension of being thrust into the lead position clouded her mind so she wasn't watching where she was going. She started to open Charlene's laptop again while she walked—and bumped head first into Babette Cooney. She bounced off the woman's enormous pillowy bosom.

Babette squealed in horror. "What are you doing, you silly girl? Keep off me with your filthy mitts."

Valerie narrowed her eyes at the ample lady. "You don't have to call me nasty names. It was an honest accident."

"You call that an honest accident?" Babette shrieked. "Why don't you watch where you're going?"

"I'm sorry I ran into you," Valerie explained. "I was just on my way...."

"I don't care where you were on your way to," Babette snapped. "Don't you think I'm on my way somewhere, too? You were looking at your computer. Don't deny it. I saw you as clear as the nose on your face."

"I admit I was preoccupied," Valerie began.

Babette clenched her fists around her dozens of bejeweled rings. "Do everybody a big favor, little girl. Go sit down in the library with your computer and leave the investigating to your big sister—wherever she is."

Valerie stiffened. "I'm in charge of this investigation now, Mrs. Cooney. You might not like it, and I can't say I like it very much, either. But Charlene — Agent Brockworth — has disappeared under suspicious circumstances. I'm worried something has happened to her. That leaves me in charge of this investigation, and I'm going to carry it out to the best of my ability, even if it is my first day on the job."

Babette reared back in shock. "Your first day on the job! Well, that's a fine how do you do. Where's that supposed to leave the rest of us? What if you arrest the wrong person? What if you hang around here for weeks without coming up with anything? This case could be dead in the water."

"It won't be dead in the water," Valerie told her. "I have some solid leads on the killer, and I just questioned Allen and the other guests in the dining room and....."

"Did you question that maintenance man?" Babette asked.

"Of course I questioned him," Valerie replied.

"Then you know he's the best suspect," Babette told her. "You don't have to bother the other guests when you have him."

"Jeff is not a suspect," Valerie countered. "He's the one person at this lodge I believe is innocent."

Babette frowned. "How can you think he's innocent? He's a ruthless killer."

Valerie shook her head. "The other guests all had suspicious business connections with Porteus Patterson. They all lied about their connection with him in relation to his death."

Babette threw up her hands. "How many times do I have to tell you? That maintenance man is as crooked as they come. He's probably been stealing things from the guests' rooms for years. I don't know why Allen keeps him around. He must be desperate for anyone who would stay up here on a long term basis."

"What make you say that?" Valerie asked. "He's got a spotless employment record. Allen is probably grateful to have such a dedicated employee."

"Dedicated? Ha!" Babette shot back. "He's dedicated to pilfering expensive jewelry and God knows what else. I wouldn't trust him within a mile of me."

"You keep saying he pilfered from the guests," Valerie pointed out. "What proof do you have of that?"

"I caught him at it," Babette replied. "I caught him in Porteus Patterson's room."

Valerie stiffened. "What was he doing there?"

Babette waved her hands in circles. "That's what I'm telling you. He was breaking into Porteus's room."

"Did you report him to Allen?" Valerie asked. "Did you lodge a formal complaint against him? If you didn't, no one else would have known about it."

"I reported him," Babette replied. "I complained until I was blue in the face. You can't run a lodge like this with an employee breaking into guests' rooms."

"So why didn't the complaint show up on Jeff's employment record?" Valerie asked. "Allen claims Jeff has always been a model employee."

Babette fixed Valerie with her eagle eye. "What kind of investigator are you? How does our government ever expect to stop hardened criminals from killing innocent citizens if they send investigators like you to solve the crimes? Don't you see? They're working together. He let the maintenance man rob his guests so he could take a share of the profits."

Valerie crossed her arms over her chest and leaned back. "Come on, Babette...."

"How dare you call me by that name?" Babette shouted. "If you can't call me Mrs. Cooney, then don't talk to me at all."

"I'm sorry, Mrs. Cooney," Valerie replied. "But you have to admit that story doesn't make sense. Why would Allen want to spoil his sterling reputation for service to his guests?"

"How do you explain the maintenance man being in the room?" Babette asked.

Valerie regarded her with her head on one side. "I can't."

Babette jabbed her finger in Valerie's face. "That's what I'm saying. Keep your eyes on that maintenance man. He's the killer if anybody is."

She sailed away somewhere. Valerie froze when she spotted the burly man following her. Who was he? She had to ask Allen about him. He must be Babette's body guard or something, although she wouldn't really need one at this lodge. Then again, Porteus probably didn't think he needed one, either, and look what happened to him.

Valerie continued down the hall. She had more than enough to keep her occupied with this case, and she still hadn't had dinner. She couldn't go back to the dining room, though. She would get room service in her room later while she went through the lab reports from the coroner. She knew the cause of death, but the other lab reports and chemical analyses usually contained valuable information about the victim. Even the contents of his stomach could shed some light on his last hours alive.

Chapter 9

She took Charlene's computer to her room and set it up on the table. She scanned down the Coroner's Report, but didn't see anything out of the ordinary. Reams of spectroscopic data and DNA testing results crowded the file.

Valerie closed her eyes and pressed her knuckles against her eyelids. She should give up trying to solve this case herself. She would call Colonel Tomlinson in Denver and get him to send out a senior Strikeforce Team member to take over. He wouldn't be too happy about a junior member trying to solve the case alone. He would read her the riot act for failing to report Charlene missing sooner.

She kicked her chair out of the way and paced around the room. She just couldn't make herself pick up the phone. She stopped at the window and gazed down at the dressage ring. Jeff crossed her line of vision, but he didn't see her. What if Babette was right about him? What if every word he'd told her was a lie? What if he'd charmed her with his clear eyes and direct stare to hide his criminal activities?

Could he really be the killer? Could he be romancing her to cast suspicion on the guests? Of course Allen wouldn't include Babette's complaint in his record if he stood to gain by covering it up.

He would take his share of the guests' valuables as long as he could safely blame Jeff for stealing them.

Maybe they worked together to kill Patterson, too. Maybe they both worked for some other underworld organization, and Jeff used his paramilitary training to murder Patterson. She paced back to the computer and had put her hand on the cover to close it, when her eye landed on an obscure line far down the page.

The Coroner's Report listed each organ in Patterson's body one after the other, including its weight and a complete chemical breakdown of the blood found inside it. The heart looked normal, but the lungs caught her attention. The read-outs for the right and left lungs weren't identical. She scrolled farther down and found the reason. Porteus Patterson had tubercular tissue in his left lung from a bout of tuberculosis. The disease was no longer active, which meant he'd received treatment and been cleared of the disease. His left lung was half the size of his right one.

Then Valerie noticed something equally intriguing. The Coroner had found traces of plant material in Patterson's lungs It was jammed so far down his windpipe that the Coroner had to bisect the cricoid cartilage with a scalpel to get it out. He identified the material as rose petals.

Valerie's heart fluttered. This was the smoking gun. Patterson was suffocated with rose petals. The irony! Now where could they have come from? She put out her hand one more time to close the computer when the last item in the Coroner's chemical analysis caught her eye. Patterson's right lung contained traces of carbon monoxide. Now where could that come from?

Then she saw it, confirmation. Microscopic traces of chloroform dotted the right lung tissue, barely enough to notice. Half a part per million. That wasn't enough to kill him. It was barely enough to report. But it was there. So Patterson had been murdered after all. Someone knocked him out with chloroform and left him in the power station room. The chloroform wore off, but by that time, the killer had stuffed rose petals down his throat and killed him. The killer got away before the power station door locked with Patterson inside.

Valerie raced out of the room. She had to take another look at the power room—alone this time. She peeked around the service door to make sure Jeff was nowhere nearby, but he would still be down at the stables.

He could be down there for hours before he came back up to the lodge, and he would be on the opposite side of the building from the power station.

She ran through the azaleas and zipped around the corner. She stopped when she came in sight of the windowless chamber with its big black door. The timer lock hummed inside the door. She'd forgotten it would be locked at this time of day. She couldn't see inside it.

A rustle in the bushes caught her attention, and the hair stood up on the back of her neck. She hurried away, but she swore that there were soft footsteps following her through the undergrowth. She headed back to the lodge. Jeff wouldn't be able to follow her there.

Her mind raced, along with her feet. Was Jeff the killer? Had he come to get rid of her the same way he got rid of Charlene? How could she trust him? What was she thinking?

She should have listened to Charlene when she warned her about falling head over heels for a man she knew nothing about. Charlene knew so much more than Valerie ever would about murder cases. Maybe she could see that Jeff was guilty the moment she laid eyes on him. While Valerie was making up her mind that Jeff was a Boy Scout and a guardian angel, Charlene could see right through that virtuous disguise to the cold heartless killer underneath.

As Valerie picked up her pace, she patted under her jacket, but her heart sank when she remembered she'd left her service pistol in her room. She'd taken it off when she and Charlene sat down to work, and she'd forgotten to put it back on. That was another rookie mistake Charlene wouldn't make. As soon as she got back to the lodge, she would call Colonel Tomlinson. This case was no way for her to start her time on the Strikeforce Team. She needed an older, experienced partner to guide her.

She heard a snap behind her. Valerie ran. The faster she ran, the faster the pounding of her heart filled her head. Could she ever outrun the killer? She spotted the steps up to the deck, and just beyond them stood Jeff.

Valerie gasped out loud. He wasn't following her after all. If he wasn't following her, who was? She ran toward Jeff. Whoever was following her — wouldn't come near her as long as she was with him. She was in over her head. Had someone been following her at all, or was she just imagining things? A she approached Jeff, a sudden surge of hope washed all her fear away. She could run toward him for the rest of her life and never lose hope. He couldn't be the killer.

She couldn't feel this kind of attraction for him if he was. Her heart and soul couldn't be that wrong.

She almost burst out laughing and sobbing in pure relief as she reached him. He smiled at her, and she raced up to him, still out of breath.

"There you are. I was looking for you."

His eyes widened. "What were you looking for me for?"

She gasped for the last mouthfuls of air. "I wanted to ask you.... I mean.... I only wanted to see.... I mean...."

He waited. She glanced back over her shoulder toward the bushes. "Is anything wrong?"

Valerie waved her hand. "I thought for a minute someone was following me."

Jeff frowned. Then he leapt into the bushes. The branches thrashed and snapped behind him. Valerie called after him. "Hey! Come back! What are you doing?"

He stuck his head through the foliage. "If someone was following you, we have to find out who it was."

"Maybe it was nobody." One particle of her mental clarity came back to her. Then another. What was she thinking? How could she turn her back on the evidence? He was a suspect and probably the killer. She stiffened, and the smile evaporated off her face. "Maybe I only imagined it."

Jeff ignored her. "We can track them. We can find out if someone followed you here."

Valerie snorted. "Track them? You're kidding!"

"I know how to track," he told her. "Whoever followed you would have left fresh tracks. We should be able to see them clearly enough in this soft soil."

Valerie caught him by the arm. "Never mind. I'm sure I only imagined it."

He paused. "Are you sure? It would only take a minute, and you should know if someone was following you or not."

"I thought it was you," she muttered.

His head whipped around. "Why would I follow you?"

Valerie pulled herself up straight and tall. "You lied to me."

He gasped. "When?"

Valerie shrugged. "I didn't really expect you to tell me about it. It's up to you to keep that sort of thing hidden. I was stupid to trust you the way I did."

"What are you talking about?" Jeff asked.

"You got caught breaking into Porteus Patterson's room," Valerie replied. "Babette Cooney caught you there. Don't tell me you don't remember. Allen might not have included it in your employment record, but you could have at least told me about it. Now I know you really are capable of killing Patterson. Maybe you wanted to stop him from getting you in trouble. I understand. You must have made pretty good pocket money stealing from the guests."

Jeff stared at her. Then he sighed. "Is that what Babette told you? Did she tell you she caught me stealing from Patterson's room?"

"Of course she told me," Valerie replied. "I never should have let myself develop feelings for you. I should have listened to Charlene when she warned me about you. She told me I shouldn't fall for someone I might have to arrest."

Jeff pursed his lips. "You're not going to arrest me, Valerie."

"You don't think so?" she shot back.

"Don't you think I've got the guts to do it? Do you think I'm really so soft that I would let you go free?"

"You won't arrest me because I didn't do anything wrong," he told her.

"Are you seriously going to stand there and tell me Babette didn't catch you in Patterson's room?" Valerie asked.

"Do you really expect me to believe she made the whole thing up to get you into trouble? She reported you to Allen. How stupid do you think I am?"

"I don't think you're stupid," Jeff replied. "Babette did catch me in Patterson's room. She's telling the truth about that."

"There you go." Valerie pointed at him. "So it's all true. You were robbing the guests."

"I was not robbing the guests," Jeff countered. "She reported me to Allen, and she would never believe I wasn't stealing from Patterson."

"Then what were you doing in his room?" Valerie asked.

"I was fixing the internet cable," Jeff replied.

"That's why Allen never included Babette's complaint in my employment record. Allen told me to go into Patterson's room, and he let me in with his master key. When I told Babette that, she wouldn't believe me. She thought I made that story up to hide what I was really doing."

He raised his right hand. "I never did anything wrong, and I swear to you, Valerie, on my sacred honor, I never had anything to do with Patterson's death."

Valerie hesitated. He gazed straight into her eyes, but that meant nothing. A Navy SEAL like him would know how to lie with a straight face. "And you expect me to believe that?"

Jeff took a deep breath. "Listen, Valerie. I can't make you trust me, but I'm telling you the truth. You're all on your own up here with a killer on the loose. What are you going to do? You don't have to go it alone when we could work together to solve this crime. You know in your heart of hearts I am who I say I am. I didn't kill Patterson, and I'm the only person here who can help you find out who did. Trust me, Valerie. Trust yourself for a change, and let me help you."

Valerie regarded him. The same sense of certainty she'd experienced when she first saw him pushed her mistrust and anxiety away. Every fiber of her being told her that he was sincere. Trusting him meant trusting her own instincts. Her gut told her he was honest and true. If she couldn't trust that, she had nothing left in the world to trust.

Her shoulders relaxed. "All right. I'm trusting you. But if you betray that trust, so help me...."

Jeff smiled. "Good. Now let's get to work."

Valerie frowned. "We've got a problem."

"What's that?" he asked.

"The Three Musketeers," she replied.

He snorted with laughter.

"The what?"

"That's what I'm calling Heinrich, Dempsey, and Andrea," she explained.

"You were right. They're always together, and they were all involved with one of Patterson's front companies. I'm convinced they were mixed up in his illegal activities, and they used this company to cover it up. They must have come up here to meet and discuss their business."

"What about Babette?" Jeff asked.

Valerie put her head on one side.

"What about her?"

"What connections have you found between her and Patterson?" he asked.

Valerie started.

"None. I don't think there is any connection between Babette and Patterson. She's the one guest I think isn't involved in this case at all. Why do you ask about her?"

Jeff narrowed his eyes. "Did you ever ask yourself what *she* was doing in Patterson's room?"

Valerie blinked. "No. Why should I?"

"She made a big noise about me being in Patterson's room when I wasn't supposed to be," Jeff replied. "She made a point of lodging a formal complaint against me and accusing me in front of all the guests of robbing their rooms, yada yada yada. She made such a big noise no one ever asked the obvious question. What was *she* doing in Patterson's room to find me there? If she had no connection with him, what was she doing there when she found me?"

Valerie stared at him. "I never thought of that."

"There was a connection between Babette and Patterson," he told her. "I don't know what it was, but they definitely had a connection."

"I'll look up her record in the federal database," Valerie decided. "Maybe she was involved in his business, too."

Jeff jerked his head toward the lodge. "Let's go."

Valerie held out her hand. "Wait a minute."

He turned around.

"Who's the creepy guy who always follows her around?" Valerie asked.

"That's Wilbur Watkins," Jeff replied.

"Is he her bodyguard or something?" Valerie asked.

"Not that I know of," Jeff replied. "As far as I know, they're just good friends."

Valerie's eyes widened. "Good friends? He's like her shadow."

He took a step closer.

"Did you know they share a room? They've been up here every year for ten years, and they've shared a room every year." He dropped his voice to a murmur. "They've shared a room with one bed — if you know what I mean."

"Then they must be a lot more than friends," Valerie pointed out. "But that doesn't give us any connection between them and Patterson."

"Let's go see what your database has to say about it," he told her.

Chapter 10

Jeff leaned over Valerie's shoulder and examined the computer screen. "There's no mention of Fidelio Transport. She must be clean."

"I wouldn't call her clean," Valerie countered. "Any one of these other income sources could have been connected with Patterson. He had dozens of front companies. Fidelio Transport was only one. Babette didn't meet with the others, so I guess she wasn't connected to them, either."

"Can't you do a cross-reference?" Jeff asked. "Cross-reference Babette's file with Patterson's. That will turn up any connections."

"I already did that," she replied. "I still come up with nothing. I also cross-referenced Wilbur Watkins. There's no connection there, either."

"There will be a connection between them in the lodge guest records," Jeff pointed out. "They were always here at the same time."

Valerie tapped at the keyboard. "You're right. But there's no corresponding connection between Babette and Patterson. They didn't come up here to meet."

"This could have been their first time," Jeff pointed out.

"But you said yourself," Valerie argued, "she must have had a connection with him if she went into his room when he wasn't there."

Jeff grinned. "Unless *she* was the one stealing from the other guests."

Valerie gasped. "She wouldn't do that. Look at her jewelry. She doesn't need to steal. She's got enough money of her own."

"Most kleptomaniacs don't need the money," he replied. "They do it for the thrill."

"You're stretching it a little, aren't you?" she asked.

"Think about it," he countered. "She would have made the most fuss about me stealing if that's what she was doing. She had to deflect the blame onto me, and I was an easy target."

"Hey, take a look at this." Valerie pointed to the screen. "Babette always came up here in the spring before. This is her first visit in the fall."

"What does that tell you?" he asked.

"Well, Patterson nearly always came up here in the fall," Valerie explained. "He was an avid hunter. He rarely came any other time of the year. But after the time she found you in his room, she changed so she would come up in the fall, too. Maybe she did decide to come up here to meet him. Maybe this doesn't have anything to do with dirty business. Maybe they had something going on."

"What about Wilbur?" Jeff asked. "Wouldn't he get jealous if someone moved in on Babette?"

Valerie grinned over her shoulder at him. "Maybe he did." She stood up. "I have an idea."

"Where are you going?" he asked.

"Babette said she didn't want to stay in a room near the power station," she replied. "She made a scene in the lobby when Charlene and I first walked in about moving to another room. I'm going to see the room she moved out of. We might find something there to give us a clue."

"Allen will have had the room cleaned by now," Jeff told her.

"Maybe. I'm going to look anyway." She started for the door when she paused and turned to Jeff. "I'd appreciate you coming with me."

"I wouldn't miss it."

He took a step toward her, and Valerie noticed the fine grain of his skin. His lips hovered before her eyes.

"I'm glad you decided to trust me. I don't think I could stand you thinking I was the killer."

She couldn't take her eyes off his face.

"I knew you weren't a killer. You're too good for that."

His eyes skimmed down to her mouth and back up to her eyes.

"You're good, too."

It felt like a bolt of lightning seared down Valerie's neck and chest and burned deep into that pit of desire between her legs. If he came much closer, she wouldn't be able to resist him. Waves of passion pulsated between their bodies. All this talk and running around only created so much static, keeping them apart. With that gone, only bare ravenous desire radiated back and forth between them.

"Jeff...." she began.

He didn't hesitate. He pulled her to him, and his body overwhelmed her. She couldn't hold back the rising tide, and she melted into his arms. No matter that there was a bed not far away – it was too far. They toppled onto the floor, tangled together in locked desire. His lips devoured hers, his tongue penetrated her mouth, and his weight crushed her into the floor.

Valerie succumbed to the rapture of his embrace. She closed her eyes and let everything outside that room slip away into oblivion. She opened her mouth to receive him, and their hands puled at each other's clothes to reveal the living skin underneath. Their bodies touched, and the waves of bliss swept Valerie into a fathomless ocean of warm black shadow.

An hour later, they lay entangled in one another's arms on Valerie's bed. Valerie closed her eyes and inhaled his earthy smell. Every cell of his body spoke to her of contentment and peace.

"Don't you want to check out that room?" he asked. "The longer we lie here together, the more likely it is we won't find anything when we get there."

Valerie sighed. "We'll get there. This is more important right now."

Jeff laughed. "You're some piece of work, aren't you? You're supposed to be a hardened investigator."

"I can't be hardened," she replied. "I just started. Anyway, I don't want to check out the room without you. I don't want to do anything without you."

He kissed her hair. "I feel the same way."

Valerie laid her hand on his arm.

"I mean it, Jeff. I don't think I could face this case by myself. I'm sorry I accused you of stealing from the guests and all that stuff. I should have known better."

He shrugged. "Don't worry about it. You don't know me from Adam. You can be forgiven for questioning me along with everyone else. You had no reason to trust me."

"I do have a reason to trust you," she replied. "My gut told me to, and I'm glad I did."

He settled in next to her. "I'm glad, too. I didn't know how boring my life up here was, until you showed up. I don't think I can go back to being a maintenance man."

"What will you do instead?" she asked.

"I don't know," he replied. "Maybe I'll go to Denver and try to get on the Strikeforce Team."

Valerie's eyes popped open. "Really? I didn't know you were interested in that sort of thing."

"I wasn't," he replied. "But now that you're here and we're working on this case together, I realize I like it. I could get used to doing this sort of thing all the time, especially if I had you for a partner."

Valerie blushed. "We won't be doing this sort of thing all the time. Besides, I'm just a rookie. Even if you joined the team, you would be assigned one of the senior agents as a partner. We wouldn't be working together."

"I don't care," he replied. "I would do anything so we could be together."

Valerie dropped her eyes. "Let's not start talking like that."

He sat up. "All right. I'm just thinking out loud here. I just wanted you to know how I felt. My place is at your side, and when you leave here, I'm leaving, too."

"When will you tell Allen that?" she asked.

"I'll tell him when the case is over," he told her. "I'll hand in my notice, and then it's back to the big wide world for me."

Valerie laughed and sat up next to him. "It's been a long time. You won't get lost out there, will you?"

He grinned. "Don't forget I'm a Navy SEAL. I can handle anything the world throws at me."

They got dressed, and Valerie straightened her hair. They shared a long, lingering kiss at the door, and then they set off down the hall. The lamps glowed on the walls, but the lodge stood silent and asleep on all sides. Valerie fought back the temptation to take Jeff's hand.

They crept down the hall in silence to the lobby and found the front desk empty. "Allen's in bed, he's not one for staying up late," Jeff told her. "If we ring the bell, we'll wake him up."

"Is there any way to get into the room without tipping him off?" Valerie asked.

"I have a master key," Jeff replied. "I'm not supposed to go into the rooms without his permission, but I could tell him you used your federal authority to compel me to do it."

Valerie made a face. "Don't pin this on me."

"How are we going to get into the room otherwise?" he asked.

"There's no one staying in the room," Valerie pointed out. "We wouldn't exactly be trespassing. I just want to look around."

"What do you think you're going to find?" he asked.

"I don't know," she replied. "Call it a hunch, kind of like how I felt about you when I first met you."

Jeff let out a deep breath. "All right. I'm willing to bet on that. Let's go."

Jeff led the way to the far end of the corridor and produced a gold key from his pocket. It shone in the lamplight. "This is it."

Valerie looked around. "No wonder Babette didn't want to stay here. This is the room closest to the power station."

Jeff pointed to the very end of the hall. "That service door leads right to it."

"That would make it pretty convenient for Babette to lure Patterson to the power station," Valerie remarked. "She could leave him there and beat a hasty retreat back to her room."

"Or," he pointed out, "Wilbur could have done the same thing."

"What do you know about him?" Valerie asked.

"Only that he's married," Jeff replied. "He's married to someone other than Babette Cooney."

"How do you know?" she asked.

"Allen told me," he replied.

He slid the key into the lock and turned the knob. The door swung open on the deserted room, and Jeff flicked on the light switch. Light flooded the room, and the stark white walls blinded Valerie. She squinted into the room and caught her breath. "Allen hasn't had it cleaned up yet."

Jeff shook his head. "That's not like him at all. He usually has a room cleaned as soon as the guest moves out. He leaves all the rooms spotless for the next guest."

"Maybe Babette took him by surprise with her demand to move to another room," Valerie suggested. "Besides, I've been asking questions and dragging him off to the dining room with me to question the others. He may not have had time."

Jeff studied the room. "That never stopped him before. I wonder what's gotten into him."

"Babette sure left a mess." Valerie scanned the room with her investigator's eye. Random papers and chocolate wrappers littered the dresser.

A crumpled tube of toothpaste sat in the trash can along with an assortment of tattered receipts. Something about them caught Valerie's eye. She picked out one of the receipts and studied it up close.

"Well, I'll be."

"What is it?" Jeff asked.

"It's one of those little cards from the florist," she replied. "It says, '*To my love, Babette. For all the years to come*'."

"Does it say who it's from?" he asked.

Valerie shook her head. "It could be from Patterson."

"It could be from Wilbur," he countered.

Valerie gave him a sour look.

"It could be from anybody. Why do you keep coming back to Wilbur, anyway?"

"Call it a hunch," he replied.

Valerie snorted. "That's my line." Then she cocked her head to one side and opened her computer. "I've got an idea. You see? I knew it. Here's the receipt."

"What receipt?" Jeff asked.

"There's a transaction in Patterson's personal credit card statement," Valerie told him. "He bought two dozen long stemmed roses three days before he died, had them delivered to the Mackenzie Lodge the same night. He had something going with Babette."

"Do you think she killed him?" Jeff asked. "What about jealous Wilbur?"

"We have no proof Wilbur was jealous," Valerie argued. "If he was sneaking out on his wife to meet Babette, she could have been sneaking out on him to meet Patterson. They could have had a very amicable triangle relationship for all we know."

Jeff grimaced. "I doubt it somehow."

"Me, too," Valerie replied. "And Patterson was suffocated with rose petals being shoved down his throat. That sounds pretty jealous to me. But it still leaves us with the burden of proof. Who are we going to pin this murder on and how are we going to pin it on them?"

"Maybe we could pin it on both of them," Jeff suggested. "Whatever we do, we'd better do it fast. Babette and Wilbur are scheduled to check out in the morning."

"Where are they now?" Valerie asked.

"They'll be in their room," Jeff replied.

"You mean the Equestrian Room?" Valerie asked.

He broke into a big grin. "That's the one."

Valerie closed her eyes and turned away. "I shudder to think what it looks like."

"I can tell you what it looks like," Jeff replied. "It's a big timber-lined room with vaulted ceilings, a big his-and-hers walk-in closet, twin hot tubs and a big balcony with a beautiful view of the dressage ring and the stables."

Valerie stared at him. Then she slapped her forehead. "That's it! No wonder they wanted to change rooms."

Jeff frowned. "What?"

"Don't you remember?" Valerie cried. "The east wing of the lodge overlooks the stables. I remember seeing that balcony when Charlene and I went to look at the chiller. The hedge around the kitchen yard is right underneath the balcony."

"Yeah?" he asked. "So?"

"So," she replied, "Babette could dump the roses from the balcony, and they would be hidden by the hedge. She had to find a way to hide them, so people wouldn't know she was having something on the side with Patterson. She couldn't even let Allen know about it. He might let the information slip to me and Charlene."

Jeff frowned. "But that means...."

Valerie grabbed him by the hand. "Come on! We don't have a moment to lose." She dragged him off to the other side of the building.

"What's the big rush?" he asked.

"Don't you see?" Valerie cried. "Charlene went to look around the lodge right before she disappeared. She must have been poking around under the balcony and discovered the roses. Maybe she even caught Wilbur or Babette dumping them. They must have grabbed her to stop her from finding out the truth. If she's still alive, they might have her tied up in that closet of theirs."

Jeff stumbled after her. "You can't be serious."

"If she's still alive," Valerie replied, "we have to find her as soon as possible. She could be dead already, but if she's not, every minute brings her closer to death. They won't leave her alive when they leave the lodge."

Chapter 11

Valerie dragged Jeff past the empty reception desk towards the kitchen. At the entrance to the servants' quarters, a wooden sign on the wall pointed up the stairs: *Equestrian Room*. Valerie let go of Jeff's hand. "Get out your master key."

His eyes popped open. "What for?"

"We're going into that room," she declared.

"Isn't that highly illegal?" he asked.

"Not when we have reasonable suspicion an agent's life may be in danger," she replied. "If Charlene isn't in that room, she's almost certainly dead somewhere on the property."

"Don't you at least want to go behind the hedge to see if the roses are there?" he asked.

"They won't be," Valerie replied. "Wilbur and Babette will have found some other place to hide them after they kidnapped Charlene."

"Do you really want to risk your career to find out if you're right?" he asked.

"I would risk a lot more than that to save Charlene," she replied.

Jeff nodded and took out his keys. "All right. I'll back you up. Let's go."

Valerie pulled her service pistol from her holster and took a firm grip on it. Jeff led the way to the top of the stairs and held his key ready. Valerie stood back with her pistol aimed at the floor.

"As soon as you get the lock turned, get out of the way. I'll go in first. You stand back until I tell you it's clear."

He threw back his shoulders. "I'm not going to stand back. I'm going in right behind you."

Valerie hesitated. Then she nodded. What was the point in arguing anymore? They were going balls to the wall on this one — no safety net, no proof, no back-up, no nothing. If Charlene wasn't in that room and Valerie couldn't prove either Babette or Wilbur or both of them killed Patterson, she was finished. She might as well pack up and go back to the Alleycat Boarding House in defeat. No other law enforcement agency on the planet would have anything to do with her.

But at least she would have Jeff. If she lost everything else, at least she would have gained him. She would never squander the gift of his support again. She would be anywhere he would be. Her dream of joining the Strikeforce Team paled in comparison to her connection with him. He was ten times the partner Charlene was. He was a life partner, and he could share so much more of her dreams and her time and her being than anyone else could.

Valerie never saw anyone work so fast. He shoved the key into the lock, and in a flash, the door swung open. Valerie strode into the room with her pistol raised.

Wilbur and Babette sat on deck chairs on the balcony, and they jumped up when Valerie swept into the room. Wilbur started forward. "Hey! What do you think you're doing?"

Valerie took aim at his chest. "Stay right where you are. Don't move a muscle, or I'll drop you where you stand."

He froze with his mouth open. Babette gasped out loud. "What is the meaning of this?"

Valerie glanced around, when a voice called from behind her. "Over here."

She looked over her shoulder. Jeff pointed toward the bedroom. Through a lofty timber archway, a grand bedstead constructed of gleaming round logs occupied the central position of an enormous bedroom. Both sides of the bed were rumpled. Valerie noticed that right away. Two suitcases stood open on the dresser.

Jeff kept an eye on the suspects while Valerie searched the bedroom. She opened every door until she found the closet. Jeff was right when he said it was big. Valerie inched her way into it and poked at the coats and dresses with her pistol. About half a mile into it, she stopped and listened. She didn't hear any whimpering or moaning. Maybe Charlene wasn't here after all.

Then she heard it. Valerie held her breath and listened hard. There it was again, a faint hissing noise. What could it be? She crept farther into the closet. She pushed the coats and pants out of the way with one hand while she kept a firm grip on her pistol with the other. What would she find in the forgotten reaches of that closet?

She came to the back wall and listened again. The hissing definitely came from the back of the closet. She pushed the last clump of hangers out of the way and cried out loud. "Charlene!"

There, huddled on the floor in the corner behind a mass of trench coats, sat Charlene with duct tape wrapped around her head. It covered her mouth, and the hiss of her breath through her nose was the only noise in the place. Two black rings of bruised tissue surrounded both her eyes and darkened her cheeks. A crust of dried blood clotted around one nostril. Stout rope tied her hands and feet behind her back.

When Valerie moved the coats aside, she found a box of glass ampules and a towel from the bathroom sitting on the floor next to Charlene. Valerie dropped to her knees at Charlene's side and lifted one of the ampules out of its place. "Chloroform."

Valerie turned her attention to Charlene. How could she get that tape off? She pulled her multi-tool out of her pocket and opened her scissors. She cut the tape. Then she locked her eyes on Charlene. "Hold on tight, because this is going to hurt."

Charlene nodded, and Valerie yanked the tape free from her mouth.

"Are you all right?" Valerie asked.

Charlene gasped for breath. "Get me out of here, Valerie!"

Valerie laughed in relief. "Thank God you're all right. You had me worried sick."

She cut the rope holding Charlene's hands and feet behind her, but she left the duct tape hanging from Charlene's hair at the back of her neck. Charlene could cut that off herself. Charlene leaned on Valerie's arms and tottered to her feet. "What happened?"

"I don't know," Charlene replied.

"I was looking around the kitchen yard, and I went to have a look behind the hedge. I wasn't expecting to find anything. The next think I knew; I woke up here with a splitting headache."

Valerie nodded. "I thought so." She helped Charlene out to the main room, where they found Jeff holding Babette by the arm with one hand and Wilbur by the arm with the other. "What's going on?"

"You better hurry up and handcuff them," Jeff replied. "They're trying to make a run for it."

"You won't handcuff me." Babette shot a wicked glance at Wilbur. "I did nothing wrong. It was all him."

Wilbur growled back at her. "Be quiet, you fool! Don't say a word."

"No." Babette snapped. "I didn't do anything wrong. He did it all. He killed Porteus, and he chloroformed that agent there and tied her up in our closet. I had nothing to do with it."

Valerie looked back and forth between the two of them. "Why did he kill Porteus?"

"Don't you know?" Babette asked.

"He thought it was a great joke when I had a fling with Porteus. Then Porteus started to get serious. Wilbur told me to break off with Porteus, but I wouldn't. I told him I would break off with Porteus when he left his wife."

"Be quiet, you fool!" Wilbur bellowed. "Stop right now before you get yourself in as much trouble as me."

"He's right, Babette," Valerie told her. "If you say anything to incriminate yourself, you should probably have a lawyer present. Even if Wilbur did everything you say, you'll still be culpable for keeping a federal agent prisoner in your closet. You knew about that, and you didn't do anything to report it. Unless you can show Wilbur threatened your life to keep it a secret, you're still culpable."

"I don't care," Babette shrieked. "He's a devil. He lured Porteus into the power station, and then he knocked him out with chloroform."

"How did he lure him there?" Valerie asked.

Babette snorted. "He pretended to be me. He sent Porteus a note, signed with my name, saying that I wanted to meet him at the power station. I didn't know anything about it until after Allen told us Porteus was dead. When I confronted Wilbur, he laughed and said I wouldn't be meeting him again."

Valerie nodded. "Stop right there, Babette. We have to arrest you for keeping Charlene's whereabouts a secret, but if you get yourself a good lawyer, you should be able to get yourself clear of the murder charge."

"I don't care what you do with me." Babette glared at Wilbur. "Just get me away from *him*."

Valerie handcuffed Wilbur, but she left Babette free. She sat the two suspects down on opposite ends of the lobby and got out her phone. "I'll call Colonel Tomlinson. He'll send a chopper for the suspects and a Med-E-Vac for Charlene."

"I don't need a Med-E-Vac," Charlene grumbled.

Valerie held up her hand. "I'm in charge of this case, and you're a victim now. Sit down right over there and don't argue with me. I have work to do."

Charlene frowned. Then she wilted and shuffled over to the leather couch Valerie pointed out.

Valerie got off the phone and taped off the crime scene. Allen stood in a corner of the lobby and explained the situation in a whisper to the Three Musketeers.

A few hours later, the paramedics examined Charlene and four federal marshals took custody of Wilbur and Babette.

Wilbur didn't look so huge sitting handcuffed in front of the marshals, and Babette appeared to have shrunk in the last half hour. Her figure slumped in her chair, and her skin sagged on her bones. She stared down at her glittering hands, but the jewels and gold on her fingers and neck looked all wrong now.

Even Charlene looked smaller. Did Valerie herself appear smaller to others now that the case was solved? She glanced over at Jeff. He didn't look smaller. If anything, he looked bigger and more imposing next to the marshals. He chatted with them with his thumbs hooked in his pockets. He looked exactly like them. He was already one of them.

One of the marshals came over to her.

"Excuse me, Agent Inglewood. You're the officer in charge of this scene, so I'll have to get your permission to remove the suspects. I'll need your signature on the circumstances of the arrest, and as head of the chain of command, you'll have to oversee us secure the suspects in the chopper and the lift-off."

He held out a clipboard and pointed to a line at the bottom. She took the pen he offered and scrawled her name. Valerie sensed herself growing in stature next to him. She wasn't the little girl from California anymore. She was the agent in charge, at the top of the chain of command. She was going back to Denver alone while paramedics hauled Charlene, her mentor, her hero, off to the hospital on a stretcher.

"Is there anything else you need to do to the suspects before we remove them?" he asked.

Valerie cocked her head to one side. "Like what?"

"I don't know," he replied. "I only thought you might have something you wanted to say to them."

"I'd like to say good-bye to Charlene," Valerie told him. "I don't think I have anything to say to the other two." She went over to the stretcher where Charlene lay with an ice pack pressed against her cheek. The paramedics worked on her arms. One of them took her blood pressure and the other started an IV.

Charlene tried to smile at Valerie, but she could only nod. "You did it, didn't you? You did it all by yourself. I should have known."

"I couldn't have done it without you," Valerie replied.

"The only reason I was able to solve the case was because I wanted to find you."

Charlene jerked her head toward Jeff. "You were right about him. I should have trusted your instincts."

"You had no reason to," Valerie replied.

Charlene shook her head. "I shouldn't have treated you like a child. I should have known you wouldn't make a mistake like that."

Valerie dropped her eyes to the floor. "No, you were right. I should have listened to you. He could have been as bad as you said. I only got lucky that he wasn't."

Charlene sank back on her pillow. "That wasn't luck. You saw him for what he was with the first glance. I saw what I wanted to see, and I saw a killer. You looked and saw the real thing. That makes you a sight smarter than I will ever be."

Chapter 12

Valerie and Jeff helped escort the passengers to the choppers, and she gave the head marshal the thumbs up to take off. They lifted away, and Valerie watched them go with mixed emotions.

"I guess I'll drive Charlene's car back to Denver."

Jeff chuckled. "You really knocked this one out of the park, didn't you? And to think this is your first case. You'll get a medal when you get back to town."

"I don't want a medal," Valerie murmured.

Jeff's head whipped around.

"What's the matter? I thought you'd be delighted with the way the case turned out."

"I am." She peeked up at his face. "I'm not so delighted about leaving you behind. We just met, and now I'm leaving. I don't know when I'll ever see you again."

Jeff took her hand. "You're not leaving me behind. I'm coming to Denver with you."

Valerie's jaw dropped. "You are?"

Jeff nodded. "I told you I was. Did you think I would lie about that?"

"I didn't think you were lying," she explained. "But I didn't think you would leave your job behind over me. I thought that was all bravado."

He swept her against his chest in one swift motion. His hot breath fanned her lips. "I'll give you bravado."

Valerie sighed against his lips, and the familiar buzz of electricity coursed through her. "I wouldn't mind a little more of this, if you're sticking around."

He pulled her hard against him, his hips thrusting against her. "I'll do a lot more than stick around. I'll be your shadow. You'll never get rid of me."

She closed her eyes, and her being dissolved into the overpowering gravity of his presence. She could almost give up her future with the Strikeforce Team for this. "Were you serious about trying to join the Strikeforce Team? Or were you just saying that?"

"I'll do more than try to join it," he replied. "I *will* join it."

"You might find that harder than you think," she told him. "It's a very competitive team. Hundreds of people apply for every position."

"You got on the team," he pointed out. "Besides, I'm made of tougher stuff than most people. I've been through SEAL training. I can get on the Strikeforce Team if I set my mind to it."

Valerie grinned. "You sound like me."

He gave her a smack on the lips. "Exactly."

"I could tell Colonel Tomlinson about you so he expects your application," Valerie suggested. "And I'm sure Charlene will put in a good word for you."

He held up his hand. "Don't you dare say a word to Colonel Tomlinson about me."

"Well, I have to say something about you to him, don't I?" Valerie returned. "I have to explain how one of our prime suspects came to help me solve the case."

"Don't tell him about me applying for the Strikeforce Team," he said. "I like to do things myself. If I can't get on the team on my own merits, I don't want to be on the team at all."

She wrapped her arm around his waist. "I wouldn't love you so much if you did."

They shared a tender kiss. "So will you give me a lift down to town?"

Valerie started back in surprise. "Right now?"

He glanced down the hall. "Well, if you've got a few minutes, I was sort of thinking to...." He trailed off.

Valerie nudged him. "I was sort of thinking the same thing."

He stole one last look around the lobby. Allen was in his office. No one else was in sight. He grabbed her hand and hustled her down the hall. "Where are we going?"

He pushed a door open, and Valerie found herself in a hall she'd never seen before. "We're going to my room. This is the servants' quarters." A thrill of excitement shot through her. The luxury of the Mackenzie Lodge had never given her the thrill the servants' quarters did just then.

Jeff guided her through a corridor of ordinary bedrooms and bathrooms to a sparse white room. A lone double bed stood in the middle, made up with neat hospital corners and a matching pillow case, and a desk and bookshelf against the opposite wall. No pictures decorated the walls, and no dirty socks or underwear cluttered the floor.

Valerie surveyed the room. "So this is where you've spent the last five years of your life."

He nodded. "Here, and out in the gardens. It's not a bad way to live."

She ran her hand over the window sill. Not a speck of dust soiled the white surface. "I thought you'd have pictures of your family in here, or maybe some keepsakes on the shelf."

"I keep all that in here." He tapped the side of his head. "I don't need pictures to remind me. Besides, I come in here to study, so I like to keep the place as distraction free as possible."

"Study?" she asked.

He motioned toward the bookshelf, and Valerie noticed for the first time the assortment of books lining the shelves. She could just make out a textbook on Organic Chemistry, Plato's Republic, The Rise and Fall of the Roman Empire, and a Japanese Dictionary. "What did you think I was doing up here — following Harry Potter?"

Valerie blushed. "What have you been doing, getting your college degree?"

"I've already got that," he told her.

Valerie gasped. "In what?"

"Aviation engineering," he replied.

Valerie shook her head. "You're full of surprises, aren't you?"

"I like to keep my mind active," he told her. "I took this job so I could think, not so I could molder away in a forgotten corner of the Rocky Mountains. I like to challenge myself, and this is the way I do it."

She grinned at him. "I can't wait to find out what other secrets you've got hidden in your closet."

Jeff crossed the room and opened the closet. He stood back so she could see every corner. A winter parka and ski pants hung from the bar, and a set of cross-country skis stood in the corner. Other than a pair of ski boots on the floor, the closet was empty.

Valerie examined the room again. "I can't believe you've been cloistered in this room all these years. It looks like a monk's cell."

Jeff grinned. "That's exactly what it is. I never would have stayed up here so long if I'd known there were women like you out in the world. I would have run screaming from the room."

Valerie chuckled. "You must have known there were women like me out in the world. I think you've been hiding from me up here."

He took her in his arms. "I would never do that. Never."

After a moment, Valerie opened her eyes and gazed into the depths of his soul. "What if you can't get onto the Strikeforce Team?"

He let out a long breath. "I'm sure my path will become clear to me once I leave the lodge. I've got the whole world in front of me. As long as we're together, I'll be happy."

"Let's not rush back right away," Valerie suggested. "Let's take a little time just for ourselves."

"We can take as long as you want." Jeff closed the door with a soft click. No *Do Not Disturb' sign* hung from the doorknob, but that click sealed them away from the outside world more than any sign could have. He turned to face her, and nothing remained to keep them apart.

He closed her in his arms, and the barriers melted into oblivion. Valerie gave herself into the void of his presence with no restraints. Not a thought for the past or the future interfered with her passion for him. She was his, now and always, and the future could take care of itself.

Hours later, as they lay together in a film of sweat, Valerie's phone rang. She rolled into his embrace and closed her eyes. It rang again. "Aren't you going to answer it?"

"No," she replied. "I'll get the message when I get up. It can wait until then."

"It could be important," he told her.

Her eyes snapped open. "I thought you would want to lie here a little while longer."

"I do," he replied, "but you just started this job. You don't want to mess it up."

The phone didn't ring again. Valerie chuckled. "There. Problem solved."

He didn't press her again, and another hour passed before they both sat up. Valerie ran her fingers through her hair. "I could get used to that."

Jeff sat up next to her, and they shared a long, luscious kiss. "I better pack up my stuff if we're going to go." He got up and pulled on his pants.

Valerie slipped into her underwear and was just pulling on her shirt when her phone chimed again.

"Now what?"

She flicked on the screen and scrolled down. "I hate to tell you this, but I can't give you a ride down to Denver."

His head shot up. "Why not? I thought...."

Valerie nodded. "I won't be driving down. We have another urgent case, and Colonel Tomlinson, our boss, is assigning me to another partner until Charlene gets back on her feet. He's sending a chopper to pick me up. I can't take you with me."

Jeff stood up straight and sighed. "I guess if that's the way it has to be, that's the way it has to be. What's the case?"

"There's a mob battle going on right now," she replied. "Half our team is assigned to it. Charlene said I wouldn't be assigned to it, since I'm the new kid on the block, but maybe Colonel Tomlinson changed his mind. Now that Charlene is out of action, they'll need every hand on deck. I could be facing a very short initiation period."

"That sounds fascinating."

Jeff threaded his belt through his pant loops.

"What will you do?" she asked.

"I'll pack up my stuff and find my own way down to Denver," he replied. "I'm not giving up, just because you can't give me a ride. You're not getting rid of me that easily. That mob battle sounds too good to pass up."

Valerie burst into a radiant smile. "Good. So I'll see you there?"

He swept his arm around her waist and pulled her against his bare chest. "You bet. Just don't forget, okay? Don't forget how it was between us."

Valerie sank into his arms, and their lips met. "I won't forget."

The End

Don't miss Valerie's next case, in "One Bad Apple" – you'll find a taste of that book just after the 'about the Author section!

About the Author

T.K. Wilde is a long term writer, who writes both fiction and non-fiction, under a number of pen names.

A particular fondness for mysteries, action, and non-standard female characters resulted in this series – we hope you enjoy it!

Books in the Valerie Inglewood Series

The series, in reading order, is

1. Bad Moon Rising

2. One Bad Apple

3. Bad Blood

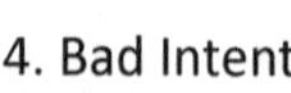

4. Bad Intent

5. From Bad to Worse

Here is your preview of Book 2 in the series

STRIKEFORCE AGENT

VALERIE INGLEWOOD

ONE BAD APPLE

T.K. WILDE

Chapter 1

Charlene Brockworth elbowed Valerie Inglewood in the ribs. "Wake up, sleepy head. The day's half over."

Valerie dragged her head off the car window. She rubbed her eyes and rubbed her neck. "Where are we?"

"We just crossed the New Mexico state line." Charlene handed her a bag of pretzels. "Are you hungry?"

Valerie made a face. "Not for that. Don't you know how bad those things are for you?"

Charlene wedged the bag between her knees. "All the more for me. We'll be stopping for gas in Taos. You can get something to eat there. Can you hold out that long?"

"I can hold out as long as it takes to get something edible." Valerie rolled down her window and gazed out at the expanse of rolling countryside. "I've never been to New Mexico before."

"This part isn't much to look at," Charlene told her. "But the rest of the state is stunning. It's especially nice up in the mountains where we're going."

"Where exactly are we going?" Valerie asked.

"You didn't tell me anything when we left. You just dragged me out of the office on a moment's notice. Is that standard operating procedure for the Strikeforce Team, or is it your idea of a joke at my expense?"

Charlene chuckled. "It isn't my idea. We don't get called up until the last minute, so when we get a case, we have to leave right away. It's the nature of the beast."

"You'd think they would at least give us time to pack our things." Valerie ran her fingers through her hair and let the wind brush it out of her face. "I didn't even get to bring my toothbrush."

"When are you going to learn?" Charlene asked. "The team sends your personal things for you. You'll get them when we get there."

"That's what you always say," Valerie replied. "So far, our things have arrived after we wrapped up the case and went home. The same thing has happened on every case we've worked on."

Charlene laughed. "That's because you're such a hot-shot investigator. You have all these cases solved in a matter of days. Most people take weeks or months to solve their cases. The team can't help it if you're a whiz kid."

"Then they should at least let me pack a bag before I leave," Valerie replied. "It would save a lot of hassle."

"I'll pass that on to Colonel Tomlinson," Charlene told her. "Maybe he'll make an exception for you."

"Good," Valerie replied. "Now tell me about this case. I don't even know where we're going."

"We're going to a spiritual retreat center in the mountains north of Santa Fe," Charlene told her. "The nearest town is a little speck on the map called Tesuque. We turn off the highway there and head into the deepest, darkest mountains. That's where we'll find our case waiting for us. The place is called EdenCloud."

"EdenCloud!" Valerie repeated. "It sounds like something an eight-year-old made up."

"Maybe they think it's like the Garden of Eden," Charlene replied. "And I guess it's up in the clouds."

"No kidding," Valerie shot back. "So what's the case? What do we know about it?"

"Cold-blooded murder," Charlene replied. "A man by the name of Harold Henderson was strangled before dinner, and everybody in the place is a suspect. That's all we know."

Valerie frowned. "That's a heck of a can of worms to find at a spiritual retreat center. Wouldn't you expect the inmates to be too pure for that?"

Charlene snorted. "Inmates!"

Valerie blushed. "What am I supposed to call them—customers? Or how about campers?"

"How about residents?" Charlene replied. "Calling them inmates sounds too severe. It's not a mental hospital, you know."

Valerie gazed out the window. "Spiritual retreat center—mental hospital—what's the difference? If they're unstable enough to strangle a man to death, they're no more spiritually superior to anybody else on the planet."

Charlene munched her pretzels. "Never mind that. Stick to the case, Watson."

"What else is there?" Valerie asked. "Do we know anything about the suspects?"

"Apparently," Charlene replied, "this Harold Henderson went by the name Firehawk."

Valerie guffawed with laughter. "That's a good one."

Charlene suppressed a smile. "It's a little unusual, I grant you. But once we get up there, we're going to have to keep it strictly professional. Get your jollies out now, sweetheart, because once we pull into the driveway, I expect you to keep your cool no matter what. Do you understand me?"

Valerie cast her a sidelong glance and snickered under her breath. "Let me guess. They all have code names. Who else have we got on the roster — Dances With Guinea Pigs? What about Dandelion Puff? Or Rottweiler Breath?" She burst out laughing again. "I can't wait to get there."

Charlene shook her head. "All right. All right. Have a good laugh. I know the names are strange, but you can't fault them for trying to improve their lives. Only one of them is a killer. I'm sure the others are good people who got caught in the wrong place at the wrong time."

Valerie shrugged. "They might not be killers, but if they pay good money to run away from the world to improve their lives, they must have some serious problems. You know the old saying. A normal person is someone you don't know very well."

Charlene shot her a grin. "If that's true, you must be as crazy as they are."

"I might be," Valerie replied. "But at least I don't go locking myself away in the mountains to fix myself. I just keep on trucking."

Charlene pulled into a gas station. "Get something to eat while we're here. We've got another two hours on the highway, and who knows how long it could take us driving into the mountains before we get there? You might not get another chance."

Valerie stared at her. "Don't tell me you don't know how far away the place is."

Charlene grabbed the pump handle. "No, I don't know. On the map they gave me, the road to the place peters out after fifty miles. I don't know how far it is beyond that."

Valerie gasped. "Fifty miles! Fifty miles off the highway? But that's...."

Charlene nodded. "See what I mean? Get in there and get something to eat."

Valerie stumbled into the gas station and came back with a grocery bag loaded to the breaking point. She set it on the passenger seat floor between her feet. Charlene came back from paying for the gas and slid behind the wheel. "What did you get?"

Valerie opened her bag. "I got some fruit and some nuts and some beef jerky and some roasted chicken legs. Do you want some?"

Charlene made a face. "Haven't you got anything with sugar?"

Valerie grabbed a bag of nuts and started crunching. "They probably won't have Twinkies and HoHos up at the center."

"No, they won't," Charlene replied. "They're hard core vegetarians."

"Hmm," Valerie muttered. "Maybe I should bring a whole roast chicken."

Charlene fired up the engine, and they drove on south through the desert. The highway wound through the foothills and through rambling towns until Charlene turned off at a deserted country store. "This is it."

Valerie looked around. "What is?"

"This is Tesuque," she replied. "This is where the blacktop ends."

Charlene dropped into low gear, and they started up a gravel road winding into the mountains. Valerie stared in wonder as the store disappeared. Everything disappeared except pine trees, scrubby bushes, and the powdery red earth under their tires.

Valerie swallowed hard and took a comforting drink from her water bottle. What if they got lost out here in the mountains and no one knew where they were? What if Firehawk's killer tried to kill them, too? This EdenCloud place probably wouldn't have cellular coverage. They might not even have the internet. Then what would she do? How could she and Charlene solve their case without basic contact with the outside world?

Clouds of orange dust billowed up from the car wheels and blocked her view of the surroundings. She had no choice but to lose herself in her own thoughts. And her thoughts invariably turned on the worst possible scenario in front of her. Who was this Firehawk? What would make a man change his name from something sensible like Harold Henderson to Firehawk? You couldn't come up with a more ridiculous situation if you tried. And now he was dead. His fellow inmates, now suspects in his murder, must be as wacky as he was.

All of a sudden, Charlene leaned on the brakes. She skidded to a stop, and clouds of dust filled the car. Valerie choked and coughed. "What's going on? Did the car die?" That was the last thing they needed right now.

"Look." Charlene pointed to a tree by the side of the road.

Valerie waved the dust away, but just as much dust surrounded them outside the car as inside. She squinted through the murk and could just make out a sign tacked to the tree. "EdenCloud. That's odd. What's that doing there?"

Charlene shook her head and threw the car into gear again. "They didn't say anything about another turn-off. Maybe someone didn't want us to find the place."

Then Valerie noticed another dirt road—more like a narrow trail—plunging down a ravine into the trees. "We're not going down there, are we?"

Charlene shifted into reverse and backed up. "What do you suggest? That we go back to Denver and tell Colonel Tomlinson that someone gave us the wrong directions so we bagged the whole case? The center must be down there, and we're going in."

Valerie gulped, and the car rolled over the edge of the cliff. She gripped the door handle until her fingers ached, but Charlene kept a firm hold on the steering wheel and her foot jammed on the brake. They plummeted down the slope, and Valerie left her last shred of hope on the top road behind them.

Find out what happens next-

Make sure to get your copy as soon as its released !

Other books from Dreamstone Publishing

Dreamstone publishes books in a wide variety of categories – here are some of our other bestselling non fiction books:-

Moving Beyond the Unspoken Grief:

A doctor's memoir of her own IVF journey as a patient

By Dr Sarah Lnyy

Should I Quit?
Resilience for a turbulent world
By Mike Gordon

"Icebreakers : How to Empower, Motivate and Inspire Your Team, Through Step-by-Step Activities That Boost Confidence, Resilience and Create Happier Individuals"

By Di McMath

All Books available from all Amazon sites and other book stores, and available for Kindle too!

And here are some of our bestselling romance books from Arietta Richmond.

Be first to know when our next books are coming out – sign up for our newsletter at

http://www.dreamstonepublishi ng.com